TAKE A CHANCE ON ME

marilyn brant

Twelfth Night
Publishing

(Mirabelle Harbor, Book 1)

DEDICATION & THANKS

For my awesome readers, who'd requested that one of my romances take place in a gym, especially after reading so many of my Facebook posts detailing my health-club adventures. "Hey Girl"...this book is for you!

Thanks to Sarah Pressly for our tagline talks over endless cups of coffee, Erika Danou for suggesting the "Pappayiannis" name, Laura Moore for being such a stellar critique partner, and each and every one of my wonderful early readers & reviewers. Ladies, I truly appreciate your encouragement and friendship.

As always, my love to my family, especially Jeff & Andrew. And my heartfelt appreciation to the fabulous women of the Glenview Book Club for six years of support and for making it a requirement that I include tasty dishes & desserts in every novel. We never lack delicious cuisine ideas to go along with our book discussions!

Finally, my gratitude to my incredible brother Joe for trying to explain the mystery of a good workout—and the various muscle groups and exercise equipment used in the process—to his far less athletic sister. Love you, Bro.

OTHER BOOKS BY MARILYN BRANT

According to Jane

Friday Mornings at Nine

A Summer in Europe

The Sweet Temptations Collection
~On Any Given Sundae
~Double Dipping
~Holiday Man

The Perfect Pair
~Pride, Prejudice and the Perfect Match
~Pride, Prejudice and the Perfect Bet

The Road to You
The Road and Beyond (expanded edition)

All About Us (novella)

The Mirabelle Harbor Series
~Take a Chance on Me
~The One That I Want
~You Give Love a Bad Name (coming soon)
~Stranger on the Shore (coming soon)

Wanderlust in Suburbia and Other Reflections on
Motherhood (nonfiction essays)

NOTE FROM THE AUTHOR

TAKE A CHANCE ON ME is Book 1 in Marilyn Brant's Mirabelle Harbor series, but this story and all of the contemporary romances in this series can be enjoyed as stand-alone novels.

CHAPTER ONE

~*Chance*~

I was heading over to the front desk of Harbor Fitness to greet my one-thirty appointment when I spotted it. The transparent cellophane wrap. The curly golden ribbons. The bulging collection of edibles. All the tell-tale signs of a gift basket from The Gala's bakery.

Aw, bloody hell. Another personal training client who was actively trying to kill me.

"Chance!" Mrs. Margot Dollinger cried, thrusting the gift of deadly delights in my face. "I wanted to give this to you as a special thanks for all of your advice in helping me recover from my shoulder injury. My range of motion is just incredible now."

To demonstrate, the fifty-three-year-old mother of four pumped her arms straight up in the air with high energy, reminding me of a fifth grader in the front seat of a plunging roller coaster.

"That's, er, wonderful, Mrs. Dollinger," I told her, through a haze of cellophane and dread. How was I going to politely get rid of this monstrosity?

1

I briefly studied the contents of the basket: Baklava dripping with honeyed syrup, cookies made with pure butter, some kind of rich custard thing in phyllo dough, and other Greek pastries I couldn't begin to identify. It was a freakin' heart attack waiting to happen.

I set the gift-wrapped nightmare firmly on the counter. "Should we get started on your final session?"

"Yes, yes," the woman replied. "And I was talking with my husband about, maybe, signing up for some additional sessions with you over the spring and summer. To work more on those delta muscles you were telling me about."

Delta muscles? I squinted at her. What the hell?

She pointed vaguely at the area around her shoulders.

Oh. "You mean the anterior and posterior deltoids," I corrected.

"Yes, them." Then with a plump index finger, she poked lightly at my upper bicep, visible to the world because I was wearing a sleeveless gray tank top—my daily uniform as head trainer at the gym. "My husband's arms don't look like yours," Mrs. Dollinger mused. "Maybe George should sign up for some sessions with you, too."

To that, I only smiled and led her toward the free weights. Some people liked to chatter endlessly. I wasn't one of them. Didn't need to be. My twin, Chandler, used to speak for both of us when we were kids, and our big brother Blake was a DJ in town. That guy did enough talking for our whole family.

In fact, the gym piped in music for us from Blake's workplace—Mirabelle Harbor's only local radio station, 102.5 LOVE FM. It was playing now. Not loudly enough, though, because even a power ballad by Guns 'n Roses couldn't drown out Mrs. Dollinger's squeals of delight and speculation.

"And how many sessions do you think it would take before George's stomach started to undulate like yours?"

Undulate? Odd word choice.

"You know," she continued. "To ripple like that?"

Ah. "The abdominals typically take some time to develop. Does your husband have a membership at Harbor Fitness or at any other gym?"

"Not yet! But don't you think that would be a really great gift to give him for our thirtieth wedding anniversary in mid-May? We're going on a Caribbean cruise to celebrate, and he could be all rippled like you by then."

I bit down on my bottom lip to keep from laughing. What was I supposed to tell her? I mean, I'd spend the better part of the past decade—from age eighteen to twenty-eight—working to refine my six pack. Being extremely dedicated to exercise and a healthful diet helped, of course. Muscle tone got harder to maintain as any man aged, though, and who knew what kind of shape George Dollinger was in at present? I doubted that anyone who hadn't made a lifetime commitment to fitness could get ripped abs (or "rippled" ones, for that matter, as George's wife had said) in six weeks or less. But how was I going to break that news to her?

"Um," I began.

"I know he could do it in record time. Especially working with someone as knowledgeable as you are," she said.

Mrs. Dollinger's expectations irritated me, but they weren't entirely her fault. Those TV infomercials that tried to convince viewers that their product could make big body changes happen fast were a total scam. Yet, people still bought into the lies. Wanted "magic." Thought high levels of fitness could be sold in stores—they just needed the right pill, the right equipment...or the right personal trainer.

I cleared my throat. "If your husband is interested, I'd be happy to meet with him and talk with him about his fitness goals." Then, before she could suggest any other super fun ideas, I handed her a pair of three-pound weights,

"Let's go over those exercises to strengthen your shoulders and upper back. The ones you did when you were here last week, okay?"

By the time she left, I was ready to collapse. Thirty straight minutes of getting pummeled by chitchat was about twenty-nine more than my brainstem could take. Thankfully, I didn't have a two o'clock appointment, so I could sack out in the staff lounge if I wanted. Maybe eat an organic protein bar and read up on some of the latest training strategies in articles from the gym's magazine collection.

When I got to the front desk, though, my coworker Gillian handed me a slip of yellow paper. "Donna called," she said.

Oh, crap.

I closed my eyes and took a deep breath. I seriously did not need this. My ex-girlfriend was...was... Well, the diplomatic way of saying it was that she was just *not* the best fit for me. Nor I for her. In any way. And don't think I didn't try to explain that to her, very gently, but with a total lack of success. I ended up having to use a lame excuse to finally break up with her.

As someone who liked to try to stay on a Zen-like even keel, no matter who I was dealing with, there were still certain types of personalities that got on my nerves. Donna's was one of them. What the hell did she want now?

I glanced at Gillian and raised my eyebrows. We had worked together long enough that she could read my nonverbal question.

"No idea what she wanted to chat with you about, Chance, but she told me she'd also called so she could sign up for one of Yasmine's classes. She had that hyper sound in her voice, like she was in the middle of some light electroshock therapy." She shrugged. "Good luck."

I groaned. Audibly.

My coworker pointed at the giant gift basket, still

4

sitting on the counter. "I'd have a few Greek pastries before you call her back if I were you. You'll need the sugar rush to keep your energy up."

Now I scowled. Gillian was just joking but, in a way, she was probably right. I'd be damned if I'd resort to using unhealthy eating habits to deal with toxic people, though. However tempting.

I pushed the basket closer to her. "Take this health hazard and put it *anywhere* else."

"Can I have a piece of baklava first?" Gillian asked with a grin.

"You can have the whole bloody thing if you want it. It's your poison."

She laughed. "Thanks, but I promise to share with the rest of the staff. This is too sweet to go to waste."

The Pappayiannis family that owned The Gala, the town's Greek restaurant and bakery, were supposedly nice enough folks. At least according to other people.

In my opinion, though, they were loud, overly demonstrative, constantly emotive, and up to their eyebrows in syrupy products. The whole lot of them were like a bunch of kindly crack dealers, and they were headquartered just down the street from the gym. There should've been a city ordinance against something so counterproductive.

I'd made it my mission to avoid sugars and sweeteners, period, but there was no way I'd ever try most of The Gala's savory items either. (Okay, *maybe* their small Greek salad, if forced.) Whenever I looked in their food display case, the words "High Fat!" and "High Cholesterol!" all but flashed at me in neon.

"Enjoy," I said to Gillian, waving at her as I walked out of Harbor Fitness and into the April afternoon.

Once I'd stolen a lungful or two of fresh air, I reread the yellow slip of paper.

Tell Chance to give me a call. Pronto. ~Donna

What would the drama be this time?

I pulled out my cell phone and punched in Donna's number. Might as well find out, although I couldn't help wishing—like the gift basket—that I could just wrap her up, stick some ribbon on her, and hand her over to someone else who'd appreciate her more than I did.

~*Nia*~

"Ow, my back," I moaned. I massaged my lower spine and the all the muscles around it, but I just knew I was going to need more professional help.

"The problem is two-fold, Nia," my doctor had told me that morning. "You need to stop doing whatever it is that caused your lower back strain, and you need to strengthen your core muscles to help prevent any further injury."

So, okay, I had a terribly bad habit of hunching over while helping to make the various pastries at my family's restaurant. There was so much detail work involved that I always had to lean close to the tray, use precise hand movements, and concentrate on the fine-motor tasks. Of course I should have remembered to adjust my posture and take hourly breaks, but I never seemed to think of it until my back started to ache.

Now I'd gone and strained it, and I'd have to figure out a way to fix myself up as soon as possible. It couldn't happen again. Demand at The Gala was high, and my parents needed my help too much for me to quit.

I curled into a comfy position on the sofa (or as close to comfy as I could get under the circumstances) and speed-dialed one of my old high-school pals. The one who seemed to know just about everybody in town.

"Donna?"

"Long time, no chat! What's up, Nia?"

So I told her about my back injury and what my doctor had suggested. "I was hoping you might know someone who'd be good at personal training. I need just a few sessions to get my 'core' muscles on track. Someone who really knows what they're doing so I don't make the strain worse."

"The obvious choice is Harbor Fitness," Donna said, slightly out of breath. It sounded like she was climbing up or around something. Or, maybe, at a spinning class? Then again, Donna was always on the move, like a coyote on the hunt. She was high energy. Even when we were teens she never could just hang out and chill.

"I thought of that," I began, "but—"

"It's close, it's convenient, it has lots of personal trainers, and I know most of them."

Despite the fact that Harbor Fitness was only a block away from The Gala, I'd never set foot in the place. It was filled with those annoying hard-body types. Guys who spent half of their free time working out and the other half admiring themselves in those massive wall mirrors.

I totally didn't need that sort of vanity in my life.

Besides, I always felt *squishy* around men like that. Knew they had to be judging my appearance, calculating every percentage point of body fat, and comparing me to the gym bunnies who were their female equivalents on the treadmills and elliptical machines. The ladies who always seemed to wear an overabundance of skimpy Lycra in a variety of pastel shades. Donna was one such person. And though I liked her, she and I didn't have all that much in common.

"I don't think I can handle working out with anyone who's leering at my chest or who's constantly talking at me, like I'm a contestant on some 'extreme' weight-loss show," I said.

The one other time I'd gone to a gym, it was during college. The trainers that were tramping through the place acted like zealous cheerleaders. They all said things like, "Keep on sweating!" and "You can do it. Just one more rep!" I'd hated every single second.

And, when I was trying to leave, one of the muscle men leaned over to his no-neck buddy and whispered about me. "Check out that one. She's got a rack," I heard him say. It was enough to make me fantasize about strangling him with one of those elastic exercise bands.

"Harbor Fitness has a couple of women personal trainers," Donna suggested. "Terri is on maternity leave but another, Allison, works every morning. She probably has a few openings."

"Mornings are a problem for me, unfortunately. That's when we make most of the specialty items for the lunch and dinner crowd. And we work again in the evenings, doing the prep for the early morning customers, so all we need to do when we wake up is bake the pastries." I smothered a sigh. "I need a trainer who's available in the afternoon."

"Well, unless you want to drive out of town, the only trainer I can think of that might fit your schedule is Chance Michaelsen," Donna said, with a tone that made him sound like the ultimate last resort. "Didn't I ever tell you about him?"

A vague memory of something negative floated through my brain. A series of rants by my friend about how the guy wasn't very attentive to her and that he was too wrapped up in himself. From Donna's description, he sounded like a real tool.

"A person could hardly get him to say anything," Donna continued with disdain. "He was just in his own little world all the time. I'd tell him the most interesting gossip about stuff going on in town, and he'd just stare at me. Unblinkingly. Hardly even acknowledging what I was sharing." She huffed. "So, I don't think you'd have to worry about him talking too much. If you get the guy to string more than three sentences in a row together during your entire half-hour session, I'd be shocked."

Hmm. Given my needs, that actually sounded sort of promising.

"But would you recommend him as a trainer? Is he good at what he does?"

"I should hope so," Donna shot back. "Fitness is *all* he thinks about. He actually broke up with me after only three weeks because he said he was 'too busy training for a triathlon' to have time to devote to a girlfriend. Insane! So, you won't have to worry about him hitting on you or leering at you." She paused. "I'm not even sure he's straight."

I caught myself smiling, glad Donna couldn't see me. How very like her to assume that any man who'd dare to break up with her must, therefore, be gay. But I didn't care one whit if he was or if he wasn't. As long as this Chance guy could help me strengthen my muscles and do it without spouting off lewd comments or making me feel like a troll at the gym, he'd be good enough.

Besides, I already had a boyfriend. Sort of. Even if I hadn't, I sure wasn't looking to hook up with anyone I'd meet at a *health club* anyway.

"Okay," I said. "I should just call the gym to set something up, right? I don't have to talk to him directly, do I?"

"No, just contact Harbor Fitness. The front desk has the scheduling book. I have to call them today about signups for a new Zumba class, so I'll give Chance a heads up about you, too. Tell him he'd better be nice to you. Or else."

"Oh, Donna, you don't have to do that! I'll just—"

"Hey, it's no problem. I'm glad to help. And if that prick gives you a hard time, you just let me know."

I winced. Already I was regretting this plan. How long would it take before I could get my life back to normal and not have to do anything as ridiculous and unnatural as working out with some dopey personal trainer at a gym?

CHAPTER TWO

~*Chance*~

It was just freakin' ridiculous and unnatural. All of these citizens of Mirabelle Harbor abusing their bodies this way.

Okay, yes, it *was* Easter Sunday and all, but still. How many caramel-filled chocolate eggs did one person need to devour during an hour-long egg hunt?

My family had roped me into attending this particular community event. My sister Sharlene was a force to be reckoned with, and when she wanted a Michaelsen family gathering, the rest of us came scurrying.

My eldest brother Derek and his wife Olivia were part of the town council responsible for planning and overseeing Mirabelle Harbor's Annual Easter Egg Hunt, so they were there, of course, as were their sons—James, Riley, and Peter. To the best of my knowledge, all three of my nephews had already eaten twice their body weight in candy that afternoon.

"Seriously, you've got to stop them," I said to Derek, as we watched nine-year-old Riley shove a handful of speckled malt-ball eggs into his mouth. James, age eleven, was working his way through a rainbow of jelly beans. And little five-year-old Peter was ruthlessly devouring the head of a milk chocolate bunny. "They're going to make themselves sick," I warned.

Man, I was *worried* about those kids.

But my big brother just laughed. "Glad you care, Bro," Derek said. "But you need to lighten up. This is a treat for them. Never fear. Most of the time, they eat their meat, fruit, and veggies."

"Yeah, Chance. Lighten up," my other big brother mocked. Blake, who was six years older than me but three years younger than Derek, knew better than to contradict any parental advice that our only currently married sibling might dish out. At thirty-seven, Derek was wiser than all of us and far more successful in the relationship department. And we all knew it, but I still thought this crazy sugar fest was a mistake.

Sharlene, four years older than me and having just turned thirty-two, was not about to take my side against Derek and Olivia either. Although she'd been married once (briefly), she and her ex didn't have kids, and Shar was the most indulgent auntie imaginable. She just shot me an amused sideways glance and said, "Don't you remember being a kid during major holidays?"

Problem was, I *did* remember. One Christmas, when I was about ten, I ate so many frosted sugar cookies that I spent most of Christmas Eve puking my guts out in the upstairs bathroom. Maybe some kids would just shrug that off. Would forget about it well before the next holiday gathering rolled around. But I wasn't one of those kids.

"All I'm saying is that moderation isn't a bad thing." I looked expectantly at my siblings in attendance, but my two brothers, my sister, and my sister-in-law all just laughed at me.

If Chandler, my twin, older than me by only two minutes, were here, he'd be in their camp, too. That guy ate more junk food in a week than I'd eaten all year.

But, shit, I still missed him. Especially on days like today.

He was the only person in the world who didn't make me feel as though I *had* to talk to be understood. He just *knew*.

"Anyone heard from Chandler lately?" I asked the clan.

Derek shook his head. Blake shrugged. But Shar said, "I sent him an email last week. He's in Atlanta now."

"Atlanta?" Olivia said. "When did he leave Sarasota?"

My sister winced. "It's been months, actually. Ever since he broke up with Abby, he's been working his way north. He was in northern Florida for a while and now Georgia. Maybe, eventually, I'll finally convince him to come home again."

My sister wanted all of us near home. Ever since our parents died—just a couple of years apart—she'd become extra protective of all of us. When Chandler and his longtime girlfriend, Abby Solinski, left Mirabelle Harbor a few years back, my sister was at least comforted by the fact that my twin had someone from home with him. But Chandler was restless and always on the move. The two of them had lived in something like five states before even reaching Florida. Guess Abby finally got sick of that. Much as I loved my brother, I could hardly blame her.

Olivia scrunched up her forehead with worry. "You know Marianna Gregory, right? Her daughter Kathryn went away to college this year—Michigan, I think? Well, Marianna just sold her house and is headed down to Sarasota for the summer. I should tell her to look up Abby while she's there. Maybe find out what the deal is with Chandler."

Shar was in instant agreement with this plan, as only meddling Michaelsen women could be. Always using their neighborly networking and social skills to "connect" people—whether or not they needed connecting.

Blake must've guessed what I was thinking because he smothered a smirk when he glanced at me. Derek just shot me a look that said, "Don't get involved."

Yeah. Like I had any intention of doing that.

Olivia said to my sister, "There's Marianna now!" She motioned toward a cluster of women in the distance. "I'm going to go over and chat with her. Wanna come with me?"

"I'll be right there," Shar said. "I'm just going to grab a soda from The Gala's booth, and maybe a piece of baklava. Want one?"

"Heck, yeah," Olivia said, reaching for her purse.

"It's on me," Shar said with a grin. "I'll get us a few things and meet you over there."

"What about us?" Blake said, feigning indignation.

"You men can get your own desserts," our sister informed us. "This guy wouldn't want a piece anyway," she added, spearing her index finger in my direction.

True enough.

Derek laughed, but Blake narrowed his eyes. "Not fair," he said, wandering a few paces away.

Olivia was already half way across the field when Shar turned to go. "One sec," I said to her.

She raised an eyebrow at me. "Don't tell me you want some baklava after all?"

"Of course not." But I nodded toward The Gala's booth at the edge of Eastman Field. It was swarmed with customers and at least as many members of the large Pappayiannis family. Looked like a flash mob was gathering over there.

Lowering my voice so my brothers wouldn't hear me, I whispered, "Do you know which one is Nia?"

My sister glanced at me in surprise. "Why?"

"New client. Starts tomorrow," I said simply.

"Oh." She studied the mob. My sister knew nearly everyone in town. I did not. "She's not there. But maybe she'll show up later. You can't miss her. She's got really long, really dark hair. Mid-twenties. Smiles a lot." Shar paused then sent me one of her snotty big-sister looks that she'd perfected during adolescence. "You're gonna hate her."

"Because she smiles a lot?"

Shar shook her head. "Because she knows pastries like you know fitness equipment. She's given me great advice many times on what to bring to dinner parties and various school-district functions. So, try not to be a jackass when you talk to her."

My sister took several steps away from me before she stopped, mid stride, and turned around. "I was wrong."

"Of course you were wrong," I shot back at her. "I'm never a jackass—"

"No. About Nia. She *is* here." Shar bobbed her head in the direction of the booth. "Over to the far left."

As Shar finally walked away to get her artery-clogging afternoon snack, I zeroed in on this Nia person.

Oh, bloody hell.

Of course it would have to be *her*. The woman in question was someone I'd seen walking past the gym many times, although she'd never come in. At least not as far as I knew. I'd had no idea who she was until today. I just knew that my pulse raced every single time I saw her. She looked like fucking Aphrodite.

Huh.

So, *she* was Nia Pappayiannis? *She* was Donna's good friend?

When I talked with Donna on the phone Friday, I'd mostly just listened to her jabber. (When did that woman ever give anyone else a chance to speak anyway?) But I'd been convinced that this pal of hers that I'd gotten cornered into working with was probably as high maintenance and high strung as my pain-in-the-ass ex-girlfriend. Donna had neglected to mention that her longtime friend was *gorgeous*. That seeing her would make my heart stop in my chest.

Derek suddenly took off in a sprint after his youngest son, who'd found something on the egg hunt that may not have been edible and, yet, the kid was trying to eat it anyway.

Blake strode over, nudged me, and said, "What's up, man? You look weird. Like you saw a ghost or something."

"Not a ghost," I replied. "Just something I didn't expect." *Someone* I didn't expect.

Just a Greek goddess come to life.

~*Nia*~

"And don't forget your change, Mrs. Lancaster," I told the older lady, who had already eaten half of the Greek Easter cookie—*koulourakia*—that she'd just purchased while waiting in line to pay for it.

"Thank you, dearie," she replied. "I'll be back for more later."

As soon as she left, my mother squeezed my arm and whispered, "That woman has a son."

"So do a lot of women."

"But, Antonia," Mama replied, using my full name as usual, "she has a *bachelor* son."

Yeah. I'd met Mrs. Lancaster's bachelor son—all 6-foot 7-inches of him. He towered over me by more than a foot. But that wasn't the real problem.

"He's a little too attached to his computer," I told my mom.

She squinted at me.

I tried to explain. "Although he's got a good job—" Mama and I both knew Liam Lancaster was a respected local accountant. "His real passion is gaming. He loves playing videogames. I don't." My older brother Dimitri had played pickup basketball with Liam. He knew Mrs. Lancaster's very tall son and had warned me off. "Besides,

I already have a boyfriend."

To this news, my mother just shrugged. "You talk of him, but I have not seen this person yet," she said, her soft Greek accent growing thicker as the day wore on.

"Well, Grant Jordan is great," I assured her. "You're going to really like him. He's everything I've been looking for. Good with people. Successful in business. Active in charities. And very handsome, too."

He was a tad *busier* than I would have liked, but when you were the head of an international company, like the Jordan-Luccio Corporation, there wasn't a lot of free time, was there?

Mama cleared her throat, but she didn't get a chance to speak.

"I'd like two Cokes and a couple pieces of baklava," a voice broke in.

I looked up gratefully and saw Sharlene Boyd grinning at me. I grinned back. She'd always been very friendly when she came into The Gala. "Of course," I said. "Let me grab them for you."

When I'd gotten her order together, I asked her about how the school year was going. She worked as a junior-high English teacher. With spring break over and the semester zipping by, I figured she must be looking forward to summer vacation as much as the kids.

She laughed at that. "I really am! But I do have a good set of classes this year." She motioned behind her, to the middle of the field, and her lips twisted into an impish smile. "Just heard you were going to have some workout sessions with my kid brother. I hope he'll be an excellent fitness instructor for you."

I swallowed. I'd forgotten Shar was born a Michaelsen. She'd been married and divorced and still used Boyd as her last name. But her family of origin was very well-known in town. In fact, the Michaelsen clan might even be larger than my own. I knew Derek and Olivia vaguely because of their community involvement. Shar was a regular at the bakery. And that radio DJ—Blake—I knew only by his voice. But there were nephews and twins and cousins and other relatives scattered about. It hadn't occurred to me until just now that the Chance Michaelsen that Donna had once dated could be Shar's brother.

"I, um...yes," I sputtered. "I start tomorrow." I could feel the twinges in my back, aching and pinching at the mere mention of those exercises. I'd been hunching again during the egg hunt. Neglecting to stretch.

Shar swiveled back, indicating the spot where her brother was standing. The man there looked like he was out of his element. A marble statue in the middle of Eastman Field. I could've sworn I saw Shar glance between the two of us and smirk.

She paid for her purchases and gathered them up. "Just make sure you get *all* of the attention and guidance you need during your workout sessions. That's Chance's job." Then, with a wink, she was gone.

Oh, yeah. I'll be sure to insist. Nothing like taking lessons from a stone sculpture.

"If he's really a nice boy," my mom said, picking up where we'd left off in our discussion of Grant, "you should bring him home to meet us."

"Okay, Mama. I will. Soon."

But as I glanced back into the field where the Easter Egg Hunt was finally coming to a close, I caught sight of Chance again—standing several yards nearer to our booth than he'd been before, and staring directly at me.

When our gazes collided, I felt a sudden and very intense sizzle. However cool his sculpted marble exterior might be, something hot and unexpected burned underneath. And this knowledge sent a sharp and zinging twinge through my entire body that had nothing to do with my aching back and pinched nerves.

It had everything to do with Chance Michaelsen and his

proximity to me, though.

If he could have such an effect on me at a distance like this, what would it be like when we were standing face to face?

CHAPTER THREE

~*Chance*~

"Nia?" I extended my hand to her because I was a *professional* and that was what we did when we met a new client. It didn't have anything to do with my desire to touch her. Much.

She looked at me oddly. Hesitant. Like she was afraid I'd try to out muscle her or something. So I added a slight smile.

If anything, she looked even more worried then, but she finally took my hand and shook it.

God, her skin was *so* soft.

"Chance." She stated my name rather than asked. How insane was it that I was proud of this? That she knew who I was already? Then I looked down and realized I was wearing my trainer nametag.

Oh.

"Yes," I said. "Nice to meet you." This was such a freakin' understatement it was almost a lie. I was usually only attracted to very athletic women, but Nia Pappayiannis had a different style and body type than the typical crowd

19

of single twenty-something ladies I ran into at the gym. She was all softness and curves, dressed in her very conservative white t-shirt and blue yoga pants. Other women wouldn't look hot in such a plain outfit. Nia rocked the look.

"Likewise," she said.

A long, awkward silence followed. I wasn't used to that either. Most of my clients talked my ear off from the second of introduction on. Not her.

I cleared my throat and flashed the clipboard I was holding at her. "On your questionnaire, you mentioned that your doctor prescribed at least ten half-hour fitness sessions, three per week, to work on core strength. Correct?"

She nodded.

"Okay." I pointed toward the treadmill. "Why don't we do an easy five-minute walking warm up, just to get your muscles moving, before we head over to the weights?"

"All right."

I helped her set the treadmill to a moderate walking speed of 3.3 miles/hour and showed her how to adjust the incline. It looked as though she'd never stepped on one of these pieces of equipment in her life.

"Have you belonged to a gym before?" I asked.

She shook her head. "It's not really my scene."

I was suddenly very interested to know what *was* her scene, but I didn't make a habit of asking clients personal questions, and I wasn't gonna start now. No matter how sexy her ass looked as she walked on that treadmill.

Man, five minutes lasted a long time. An eternity of unexpected fantasizing.

When the warm up was over, she trailed me to the free weights area.

"We're going to do an exercise without weights first," I told her. "They're elbow-knee touches with a torso twist. The focus is on strengthening the abdominals and all the core muscles."

I demonstrated the technique. Tightening my abs, I squeezed my bent right elbow and my left knee together until they were almost touching, exhaling. Then, on the inhale and without relaxing my stomach muscles, I pulled my knee and elbow apart, switched sides, and twisted so my right knee and left elbow squeezed together. As they came close to meeting, I exhaled. Then I repeated everything several times so Nia could copy me.

She did it. Perfectly.

"Keep your abs tight during the whole exercise," I instructed, waving my palm near her slightly rounded belly but being careful not to touch her.

Her curviness fascinated me. I was so used to seeing adults who were at the extremes—either significantly overweight and trying to put into place a more healthful regimen, or hardcore fitness enthusiasts trying to define their already well-sculpted figures even further.

Nia's body appeared firm in all of the important places, but it was the tantalizing sway to her breasts and her buttocks that made me long to cup her to me. To pull her softness against my hardness. To, at once, take her and be taken by her.

Imagining that had me abruptly turning away from her and jogging off to grab a couple of free weights, so I could take a few moments to get my dick to calm the hell down. It was like being in high school all over again. The personal trainer shorts I wore were long and baggy, but I could feel the strain against the fabric.

Note to self: No snug shorts or sweatpants on Monday-Wednesday-Friday afternoons when I was seeing Nia.

"Okay," I said, giving her a pair of yellow two-pound hand weights. "Take a one-minute break to relax your muscles and catch your breath. Then do the exercise again, this time holding the weights."

She puffed out some air, tightened almost everything

from her jaw to her ankles, and then began repeating the twists. Only problem was that her wrists were loose and they flicked backward when she made the elbow-knee connection.

Instinctively, I reached out to grab her hand nearest to me. To steady it.

She flinched beneath my fingers.

I let go of her like I was holding a burning poker. "Sorry," I said. "I just—your wrist. That position—I, um, didn't want you to hurt yourself."

My thoughts were weirdly jumbled. I had to take a few deep breaths before continuing. "If your wrists aren't held very firm as you grip the weights, Nia, you could strain them. Badly. I know you didn't come here to get more injuries."

She relaxed a little, exhaling very slowly. "Sorry for being so jumpy. This—" she motioned around the gym, "is all really new for me." And then smiled. "Thanks for coming to my rescue so fast."

My throat literally went dry. Her smile was like...pure, undiluted sunshine. The entire fitness center suddenly looked brighter, as if the blinds had been pulled back from the windows and all of the ceiling lights turned on.

"No problem," I managed.

She finished the set cleanly, using proper form, and then we moved on to the Nautilus machines. After I explained to her that the stomach muscles and the back muscles worked in tandem—that, like the biceps and triceps, you didn't want to strengthen one and ignore the other—I had her do a few reps on a couple of machines designed for stretching and toning the various regions of the back.

During a rest between sets, she shot me a speculative look. "So, I saw you at the Easter Egg Hunt yesterday. Did you enjoy it?"

"Me? No. My nephews did, though."

She actually laughed at me. "A flat-out no? Wow. It must've been bad. Why not?"

I wasn't about to try to explain the truth to the little pastry princess, no matter how pretty she was, so I just shrugged and tossed her words back at her. "It's not really my scene."

She threw her dark head back and laughed some more, the masses of long black waves falling around her face. "Well played, Chance."

Our eyes met and—damn. What could I say? I liked her. I didn't *want* to like her, but I just did. Aside from being so incredibly hot, she was sweet and funny and...different from what I'd expected. Especially given her friendship with Donna.

The thought of which was like being hit with freezing cold water. *Stay away from women who are friends with your exes. Common sense, dude.*

"So, uh, did you and your family have a good Easter?" I asked.

She looked fleetingly amused. "For us, it hasn't happened yet. We celebrate the Greek Easter, so our holiday won't be until this coming Sunday."

"It's different?"

She nodded."We follow the Christian Orthodox tradition, which uses the Julian calendar rather than the Gregorian one. Every once in a while the holiday falls on the same day as the Western Easter, but it's often a week or more later."

"Interesting."

"I don't think I've ever seen you in The Gala, Chance. If you stop by while I'm working, I'll give you a couple of our traditional Easter cookies to try."

"That's, uh, nice of you, but I'm fine."

An odd, confused look crossed her face. "What are you saying? That you don't *want* to try them? Don't you *like* cookies?" She seemed to consider this an impossibility.

23

"They're just always packed with fat and sugar," I blurted, which was unlike me. I never spoke without thinking, but Nia had me rattled this afternoon, personally inviting me into her family's bakery and all. "No offense," I added, "but I'm very cautious about what I eat."

Her expression morphed from being mystified to something less easy to identify. *I* couldn't read it, in any case.

"Yeah, Donna said you kept to a very restrictive diet. Because of your triathlon training, wasn't it?" She raised a dark eyebrow as if she'd guessed my breakup line had been at least slightly exaggerated, if not an all-out fib.

"Exactly. My *training*," I said with emphasis. I'd actually given Donna a handful of reasons for ending our relationship, my careful dietary choices were just one of them. (Donna loved dining out.) But it also happened to be true that I didn't eat junk food. Most restaurants were pretty accommodating when I made special requests. I just didn't like to have to ask.

"Well, there are a lot of good-for-you Greek foods," she informed me. "The Mediterranean diet is known for promoting longevity and healthfulness. Veggies are a staple. Lean proteins, Omega-3 fats, olive oil, and fresh fruit are commonly used as well."

As are butter, phyllo dough, and sugar, I added silently.

"I imagine it's all very...tasty," I said instead. *Look at me, being so diplomatic!*

"You shouldn't just *imagine*," she shot back. Then she grinned, as if laying a trap. "Don't judge a cuisine until you actually try it. I'll bring you a piece of *spanakopita* on Wednesday, and you can taste it for yourself."

What the hell was *that?*

My longtime rule was that if I couldn't spell or even pronounce a food, I wouldn't eat it. Just. Say. No.

I started to shake my head.

"It's a spinach pie," Nia said. "There are onions, feta

cheese, herbs and spices, along with a lot of spinach, all of it packed between a few thin layers of pastry."

"I...um, well—" So, okay, there were *vegetables* in this thing, but still.

"You don't really know a lot about my family or our heritage, do you?" she said sweetly, but I couldn't mistake the edge of challenge in her voice.

"Guess not," I had to confess.

"Well, then, you're lucky I'll be able to enlighten you."

She finished her cool down and final stretches in silence. Then, with a "See ya Wednesday" and a quick wave, Aphrodite's slightly mischievous twin sister disappeared out the front door of the gym while I stared, open mouthed, after her.

Just who was instructing who here today?

~Nia~

This much I could tell you about the guy: He was *not* who I'd had in mind when Donna was bitching about him earlier this year.

His body reminded me of Ryan Gosling's in *Crazy, Stupid, Love.* A couple of times Chance Michaelsen moved in a way that caused the bottom of his shirt to rise up, and I caught a glimpse of the incredible abs underneath. That *omigod* six pack.

I fanned myself thinking about it and tried to keep from literally bolting out of Harbor Fitness. I crossed the street and headed over to the shady side, just to cool down.

This notion Donna had that Chance didn't pay attention was pure baloney. He observed everything. He wasn't someone who used a lot of extra words to make his point, but he listened. And he spoke when necessary.

Also—and I'd stake my life savings on this—he was NOT gay.

But he did have a weird thing with food. One of the

fitness instructors (Yasmine?) brought a birthday cake into the gym not long after I arrived. Chance looked at it as if it were infested with maggots. I almost laughed aloud at that. He sort of needed someone to loosen him up, didn't he?

But then he'd touched me, and it was like a burst of static electricity—shocking and unexpected. Seriously, that old cliché about not playing with fire? Totally applicable here.

So I should have known better than to poke at him. It was like rousing a tiger. But I couldn't seem to help myself. I'd had only a handful of serious dating relationships so, perhaps, I wasn't the most experienced woman on the North Shore, but I'd always been able to tell when a man was flirting with me. Chance Michaelsen didn't leer, but the intensity of his gaze had only strengthened since yesterday. Everything about him said *hot and hotter*.

I checked my watch. I had an hour to take a walk, work off some of this nervous energy, and just regroup mentally before going back to the bakery and working again.

Fun as it was to flirt back a little with Donna's very straight and sexy ex, this was a relationship that could go no further than the gym. Aside from the unwritten rule that a girl didn't go out with her friends' ex-boyfriends, no matter how attractive one of them might be, I could already tell that he'd be doomed (at least in my parents' eyes) as a potential suitor for me.

In an Old World Mediterranean family, you just didn't bring people into it who didn't love to eat. Period. Literally *every* member of my immediate and extended family was a foodie, and most of them specialized in some area of Greek cuisine.

My mom, my dad, my aunt and uncle in Wilmington Bay, Wisconsin—all of them were restaurant owners. My relatives in Wisconsin ran Jason's Joint (known throughout the southeastern part of the state for their gyros). And when my cousin Nick left Wilmington Bay, he moved down to

Chicago with his partner to work at a restaurant—The Playbook—and spiffy up their dessert menu with Greek delicacies. My brother Dimitri worked at The Gala, as did I. And we had other cousins, aunts, uncles, and other distant family who lived within an hour or two of Mirabelle Harbor and were the verified kings and queens of *moussaka*, rosemary roasted potatoes, lemon chicken, lamb, *tiropita*, *dolmades*, *tzatziki* sauce, and *souvlaki*.

The Gala—a name my parents shortened from the sweet Greek custard pastry known as *galaktoboureko*—happened to be one of my family's specialties. Did it have sugar? Did it have fat? Hell, yeah!

If Chance were to come waltzing into my parents' restaurant and bakery and react to its namesake by wrinkling up his perfectly formed nose and carrying on about grams of trans fats or some such nonsense, conversation in the place would stop and everyone in it would stare at him in horror and disbelief. You'd be able to hear a drachma drop.

Then the heads would start shaking, the fingers would start wagging, and Chance would be immediately dismissed as any kind of marriage material. I knew this to be true.

Which, in a strange way, was sort of a relief, I realized, as I speedwalked through the heart of Mirabelle Harbor, making a large loop around the picturesque downtown. Chance Michaelsen might have penetrating hazel eyes, but he was a guy I could write off from Day One. And that was a good thing because, to be frank, he could have been dangerous to my heart. It was more than his looks. There was just something about *him* that got to me.

Now, Grant Jordan, on the other hand, had real potential. He wasn't a committed foodie, but he had a healthy appetite for rich and exotic dishes. We'd gone out to eat at several fancy restaurants, even once to The Playbook, where we chatted with my cousin and sampled not one, not two, but *three* of their desserts, even after having eaten a full meal. He was adventurous, experimental, and not at all afraid of a little fat or sugar.

I crossed Castle Street and headed up toward Brighton Avenue—always a treat to peek in on the arts and crafts shop near there. Plus, there was a bench I liked beneath the awning of the store where I could sit down and make a call.

I pulled out my phone and speed dialed Grant's private cell number.

"Hi, you've reached Grant Jordan," the confident voicemail message said. "I can't answer at present, but your call is very important to me. Please leave me a message, and I'll return it as soon as possible."

"Hey, Grant, it's Nia. I was just thinking about you and wanted to say hello. I know it's the start of a busy week, so just give me a call when you have a free moment."

Aw, that was lame, but I'd gotten used to leaving him voicemails. He *did* answer, and usually he was fairly quick about it. But it was weird to always have to go through an electronic intermediary before being able to speak with someone I was supposedly dating.

Checked my watch again. Still a half hour left before I had to report back for cooking duty. This time away from The Gala was a much needed break. And I had to admit, I was surprised that, after just one session with Chance, my back was already feeling a little bit better.

Or maybe it was just better by comparison to the rest of my body, which had started to ache in unusual places, thanks to the exercises he'd made me do. My arms were sore from that overhead pull/press thing, and my stomach muscles were still burning in response to those seemingly endless torso twists.

I exhaled. It was a beautiful spring day, though, and I loved getting to drink in the sunshine.

My phone buzzed. Grant.

"Hello, you," I said. "That was fast."

"Hey, beautiful. What are you doing right now?"

"Just out for a stroll. Wish you could join me."

He laughed. "Me, too. More than you know, Nia. I've got the monthly investors' board meeting starting in about four minutes. It should've been called a B-O-R-E-D meeting."

As we chatted for those precious few moments, I couldn't help but imagine what life with CEO Grant Jordan would be like. He lived large, with a mansion in Winnetka on Lake Michigan and a corner high-rise office in Chicago that overlooked Lake Shore Drive. He had great tickets to some of the biggest sporting events in the city—Bulls, Bears, Blackhawks. He had a fast European-made car, a driver on call when he wanted to take the guests out in a limo, and even a little boat, which was attached to a summerhouse he owned on Nantucket. Money wasn't much of an object for Grant.

Then again, these little snippets of conversation would likely be the most I'd get from him between six a.m. and eight p.m. on weekdays. He worked long hours, which was why we only got together on Friday or Saturday nights, if at all. Time was the rarest commodity in Grant's world, not cash, diamonds, or gold.

But my mom wanted to meet him. So, when he asked if I was free for dinner this Friday, I said, "Yes. But why don't we get together in Mirabelle Harbor this time? I'd like to give you a quick tour of The Gala. Then we can go out to eat anywhere you want."

There was a long, uncomfortable pause on the line, and I worried that I'd overstepped some invisible boundary of his.

But he said, "Of course." Then, after a beat, "Should I be on my best behavior?"

I couldn't help but smile. Grant was no dummy. "There will be family present," I admitted. "My mother doesn't believe you're real, so I wanted to officially verify your existence."

Grant chuckled at that, thankfully. "I consider myself forewarned, Nia. I'll take off a little early from the office that night. How's six-thirty?"

"Wonderful."

After Grant and I hung up, I meandered down Spring Street, past the bank, and then east until I hit Cherry Avenue. Up ahead, just leaving Mirabelle Market, was a woman my parents knew better than I did, Julia Crane, the young widow of the late Dr. Adam Crane, who'd been one of the town's most well-respected family doctors. He'd died in a horrific car accident this past winter. No one's fault, as far as I knew, just icy roads and bad visibility, but it was tragic nonetheless.

She was a school teacher at the junior high—a friend and colleague of Sharlene's—and the two of them had visited The Gala a handful of times together. I hadn't seen Julia in recent months, though. Not since the accident.

I was about to call out to her, just to say hello, when I spotted a familiar figure jogging across the street toward her.

Chance.

Neither of them were looking in my direction, and when I saw them together, I fell back into the shadows of the grocery store, not wanting to interrupt.

I couldn't hear what Chance was telling her from this distance, but he was grinning at her and wrestling away from her the two or three grocery bags she was carrying. Then he walked with her across the street to the public parking lot, deposited the bags in her trunk, and took off with a light jog back toward the gym.

I knew it was daylight and I wasn't witnessing any kind of romantic tryst, but I couldn't help but feel as though I was almost eavesdropping on an intimate moment. There was something in Chance's expression that spoke volumes, even when his words didn't. A softness in those intense eyes when he was looking at Julia just now. I felt almost...jealous.

I knew the Cranes had a daughter, too. She was only nine or ten, if I was remembering correctly, so the story of Dr. Crane's death was even sadder. How hard it must be to finally find your soulmate, only to lose him so soon. I couldn't imagine the pain Julia must have gone through or the loss she and her daughter must still be feeling. I couldn't help but wonder if Chance just felt a sense of compassion and protectiveness toward her or if it was...anything more.

Julia struck me as quite pretty. Someone men would be drawn to. She had long blond hair and was still in her mid-thirties. Only about eight years older than Chance. And she was a close friend of his sister's to boot. It wouldn't be that unusual if, perhaps, he had a crush on her.

Not that I had a horse in that race. Chance Michaelsen could fall for anyone he wanted.

I had Grant (kinda, sorta), and I'd be seeing him in just four short days.

Nothing but the ticking of the clock stood between now and then, I thought to myself, as I headed to The Gala to prep for the Monday dinner rush.

Working for the weekend, to be sure, but it was going to be *amazing* once it finally got here. I just knew it. And then maybe, with my parents on board, I'd be more sure of where things stood between the venerable Grant Jordan and me.

CHAPTER FOUR

~Chance~

A few things never failed to piss me off:

People who texted while driving.

People who talked loudly on their cell phones next to me, especially at the gym.

And people who came in late to one of my sessions because they were either texting or talking.

Put away. Your damn phone. Already.

So, let's just say I wasn't in the happiest of moods when Nia arrived at Harbor Fitness on Wednesday at 2:03 p.m. with her cell phone glued to her ear.

I'd walked up to the front desk to meet her, looking forward to seeing her again, but she held up her finger at me in that "just one more minute" motion. I wasn't pleased.

Still, I waited one minute. And then two minutes. And then four. She just kept on talking. Feverishly. To one family member or another. There were arrangements being made for some kind of Friday night gathering, from what I could tell. I didn't care what the complications were. The clock was ticking.

I snapped my fingers at her to hurry the hell up.

She glared at me. "I'm trying!" she mouthed.

Pretty sure I rolled my eyes.

I turned away and began walking toward the mats—might as well start getting things set up since she was taking a freakin' eternity to finish her phone conversation—but I caught the phrase "you'll all be meeting Grant Jordan" just before I left. His name was one I recognized. Some mega CEO of plastics or something, and one half of the Jordan-Luccio Corporation downtown. What was she doing with *him?*

When she finally scampered over to me, she was breathless and apologetic. "I'm really sorry, but my aunt and uncle and one of my cousins are making a special trip down here on Friday, and I needed to give them some...um, instructions."

Ah, yes. The many talkative aunts and uncles and cousins of the Pappayiannis clan. I'd seen them hovering around The Gala before and spilling into the streets of Mirabelle Harbor. One big happy Greek family. They chatted. They gestured. They kissed each other repeatedly on the cheek. "Sounds important," I said dryly.

She narrowed her eyes. "It is." She paused and leveled her gaze right at me, like a laser beam. "I'm introducing them to my boyfriend."

"Grant Jordan is your boyfriend?" I asked before I thought better of it.

"Yes," she replied.

Damn. That was one hell of a complication.

Well, it was a good thing she was off limits—thanks to being one of Donna's BFFs and all—because, much as I had confidence in my ability to win over most women, if I set my mind to it, I also liked to think I had a healthy grasp of reality.

It'd be pretty hard to top a guy like that. Physically, sure. I mean, I could probably take him in a fist fight, but the dude was loaded. Women tended to go for flash. Can't say I wasn't a little disappointed, though, that someone like Grant was Nia's style.

"Last I checked," I told her, "today was still Wednesday afternoon, so if you've got your social calendar for the weekend all squared away now, I've got some exercises for you."

She crossed her arms and exhaled slowly. Irritated with me? Yeah, that seemed likely. But all she said was, "I'm ready."

"Good. It's about time. How's your back been feeling?"

"All of me has been sore," she retorted.

"*All* of you, huh?" I doubted that. The mental image of her up against my bedroom wall with me sliding hard into her—over and over again—flashed through my head.

I looked away from her so I could catch my breath and blink away the image, but when I looked back, there was a peculiar expression on her face. As if she'd guessed what I was thinking...and was silently measuring my ability to pound into her until every part of her was *actually* sore.

It was embarrassing, the glance that passed between us. And. So. Very. Hot.

She blushed a little, and I looked away again. I was used to having more control than this. What the hell was this woman doing to me?

Nia cleared her throat. "My arms, shoulders, upper and lower back, and hips are sore. From the torso twists and the weights," she clarified. "My stomach, too."

"All right. We're going to work all of those same areas today, but we can use a different set of exercises to do it."

I hadn't had an opportunity to tell her what I'd had in mind until now, but the workout I'd planned for her today focused on partner exercises. I knew she wasn't a big fan of the gym equipment, so I thought she might like this better. Stretching on the mats. Having a partner for weight resistance.

The only downside (upside?) of this was just how much I was going to have to touch her during this session.

"Sit on the mat," I instructed her, "and open your legs to each side so you can stretch to the front. Hands on the mat. Try to lean as far forward as possible."

She did this with ease. Hmm. Flexible girl.

"Okay, I'm going to press gently on your back and, then, more firmly, so you can get a deep stretch," I told her. "Feeling a slow ache is fine. Feeling a sharp pain is not. Let me know when you've stretched as far as you want to go."

"Okay."

As she did last time, she was wearing just a simple t-shirt and yoga pants, and the fabric of the shirt was thin enough that I could easily feel the contours of her sports bra underneath. I could also feel the delicate bones of her spine as she arched forward, and the pressure of her muscles' resistance against the weight of my palms.

This was a common stretch. I'd done it with clients a thousand times. Never before had I wanted to tear away the fabric and rub a woman's bare skin so much.

Especially when she moaned softly.

I swallowed and pulled my hands away. "Too much pressure?"

"No," she murmured. "That's really helping."

She leaned even further forward, inviting me to press harder. I caught a whiff of something floral as I moved in closer. It was like inhaling spring.

I tried to keep my mind from being flooded with images, but between the scent of her, the feel of her, and the sound of the music being piped in from 102.5 LOVE FM, it was difficult. This was Blake's time slot, and in the span of seven minutes, the bastard transitioned from playing Faith Hill's "Breathe" to Ed Sheeran's "Kiss Me" to Marvin Gaye's "Sexual Healing," which I needed to hear like I needed a charley horse in the middle of the night. One more suggestive song like that and I was gonna kill my brother.

Still not sure how I made it through the rest of the session but, by the end of it, I was cursing my growing desire for Nia and the competitive streak that had me rising to the challenge of battling the hotshot CEO for her affection. I might not succeed, but I'd be damned if I didn't at least try.

"So, Friday?" I asked, taking a step closer to her. "Same time?"

"Uh, yeah." She bobbed her head. "The afternoon still works."

"Good." I smiled at her. I'd been told I looked "very serious" more than once by clients, so I was making an effort to appear more lighthearted. Not sure it was working, though.

Her eyes crinkled in suspicion, and she opened her mouth to speak, but I saw something and had to dash away.

"Excuse me for a sec," I said, jogging over to where Mr. Alleghany was standing on the elliptical machine, struggling to step down. He was eighty-two, and I'd caught him wobbling after working out more than once.

"Let me give you a hand," I said to him, helping him down and making sure he was steady before letting go.

"Thank you, Chance," the older man said with a laugh. "Not as young as I used to be."

"None of us are, sir," I replied.

He chucked, patted me on the shoulder, and wandered away. I returned to Nia.

"Sorry. You were about to say something?"

She nodded and pulled a paper-wrapped item out of her bag. "*Spanakopita*," she explained, handing it to me. "Made fresh this morning."

"Thank you."

Her dark eyebrows rose. "You're welcome, but you shouldn't say that until you try it." Her lips curved into a devilish grin. "I'm waiting."

"What—you mean, now?"

She flashed a bunch of really pretty white teeth at me. "Well, yes. No time like the present, right? Open it up. Take a bite."

I carefully unwrapped the paper from around the *spana*-whatever and studied it. It looked very much like a pastry. "You said there's spinach inside?"

"Yes. And feta cheese and onions and spices and more." She laughed. "Seriously, Chance. It's not going to bite *you*. You need to bite *it*."

In spite of the fact that this was far from my usual fare, it seemed to be real important to her that I taste the spinach thing. So I took a small bite. And chewed. And it was...well, not bad, actually.

"What do you think?" she asked.

"It's a little richer than I expected," I said honestly, "but it's also a pretty good combination of flavors." And, because I wanted to make her happy and, also, because I did kind of like it, I took another bite. A bigger one. And nodded as I chewed.

She smiled at me in that joyful way that lit up her whole face. "Okay, so here's the hundred-thousand-dollar question—would you be more willing to try some other Greek dish now that you sort of liked this one?"

"Another savory, vegetable-heavy dish? Yes," I said decisively.

"But not a dessert?"

I shook my head.

Nia snorted. "Well, we're making some progress anyway." She took a step toward me, reached out, and brought her index finger to within a millimeter of my mouth.

I held my breath.

"You've got a little phyllo dough on your bottom lip," she said, grinning. Then she abruptly stepped back. "See you in a couple of days."

I licked my lip, captured the stray bit of pastry, and watched her glide away.

~*Nia*~

My body was tingling *everywhere*.

After the session on Monday, I'd been sore, but today...oh, God. I could still feel his hands on me. His touch made my skin want to scream, "Just. Do. It."

It was bad.

While I was at the gym, I kept trying to figure out what it was about Chance that affected me so much. There was his strength. The fact that he had all of this unexpressed power, like a wild animal in those quiet, stalking moments before he pounced on his prey.

There were his eyes, too. Those deep, golden, intensely focused eyes. And he was watching me with them. A lot. Even more than last time.

I didn't have time to take a long walk today—The Gala was catering a bridal shower tonight, so there was more to prepare in advance—but I needed to burn off some of the energy that had built up after this session at the gym. If every time was going to be like this...jeez. How was I going to make it through eight more sessions?

I decided I'd walk just as far as the bookstore down the street before heading back to The Gala. Maybe grab a romantic suspense novel for those nights when I couldn't sleep, or I might pick up a fun cookbook for my mom. She loved to try new recipes and Mother's Day was coming up.

Which in no way explained why, when I got into Between the Pages and started wandering down the aisles of the bookstore, I didn't head to either the fiction section or the area for cooking resources.

Instead, I found myself making a beeline to the "Self Help - Relationships" shelf, and flipping through a half dozen volumes.

Jaleina Longoria, the owner of this independent bookstore and one of the most well-read women in Mirabelle Harbor, finished up with the customers at the counter and then came over to me.

"Hey, Nia. What can I help you find today?" she asked.

I'd always like Jaleina, but towns like ours could be tricky. Gossip was a reality, and you didn't necessarily know who'd tell on you if you revealed something too juicy. With a boyfriend as well known as Grant Jordan and a personal trainer who was one of the über-connected Michaelsens, I had to be careful.

"I'm looking for a few things," I said, mentioning the romantic suspense novel and the cookbook I'd had in mind for Mama. "But a friend of mine is getting married soon," I added, which was only a partial lie. I was acquainted with the bride whose shower we were catering tonight, but I wouldn't exactly call her a friend. Jaleina, however, didn't need to know that.

"So, does your friend need a wedding planner or guidebook?"

I shook my head. "No, more along the lines of a 'how do I know for sure if I'm with the right guy' kind of book."

"Ah," Jaleina said gently. "She's getting cold feet. I've never been married myself, but I hear that's common." She scanned the shelves before tapping one of her long, polished fingernails on the spine of a very pink book called *When It's Hot & When It's Not: The Dating Girl's Handbook for Finding THE ONE*.

"Don't let the bright pink cover fool you," the bookstore owner said. "It's not as fluffy on the inside as it looks on the outside. There's actually some decent psychology within its pages, in between all of the usual quizzes and checklists and things."

"Great. I'll take a peek," I told her. "Thank you."

"My pleasure."

The door jangled and another customer walked in, so

Jaleina excused herself and left me alone in the "Self Help" aisle.

I opened the pink book and read the Table of Contents. There was a section on "First Impressions." Another on "Dating Expectations." Yet another on "The Role of Fear." I turned to the latter chapter and started reading:

> *"Fear about pursuing a relationship can take many forms and can express itself in surprising ways. The first question to address, however, is whether there is a legitimate basis for this fear (as in, the potential partner has certain traits that make him a poor fit for you) versus whether the fear stems from a more personal place of origin (that is, your own concerns about commitment, a lack of readiness/maturity to settle down, worry that your dating years will soon be behind you, etc.). So, to begin the analysis, you must first be willing to be completely honest with yourself..."*

I thought about Grant—did he have any traits that were "a poor fit" for me? I couldn't think of any major ones. He was sophisticated and charming, bright and funny. Though, I had to admit, we hadn't had much unstructured time together. He was busy, but I didn't get the sense that he was covering up any other activities (or women) just because he wasn't always around. He was running an internationally known company.

So, of course someone like Chance would seem by comparison much more...accessible, for lack of a better word. And watching him eat that piece of *spanakopita* today was pretty hilarious. The expressions that flitted across his face! I laughed just remembering.

Why was I so fascinated with him? A relationship

between us couldn't go anywhere and, sexual chemistry aside, it was just idle curiosity that kept me wondering... It had to be.

But why did I think of Chance every time I was *trying* to think about Grant? Why did I keep comparing the two men in my mind when, really, there was no question that Grant was the bigger catch.

The guy was a mega-star in the business world.

I'd known him for a while and enjoyed his company.

He'd asked me out several times.

He'd already told me he "really liked" me, and I said the same to him.

And he was willingly going to meet my family in two days, which was a sign of "commitment readiness." (At least according to the checklist on page 27 of the pink book.)

It had to be a case of nerves on my part, just like the book suggested. Fear that I might be close to reaching the end of my dating journey. That I may have really found "The One."

Which made me feel a lot better than some of the other alternatives—like attributing my sudden doubts about my big-city boyfriend to the far more uncomfortable possibility that Chance just turned me on a helluva lot more than Grant did.

CHAPTER FIVE

~*Nia*~

I should've known Chance would make Friday's workout session as difficult on me as humanly possible.

"You need to keep your back straight when you're doing this pull down, Nia," he informed me for probably the fifth time, an edge of frustration working its way into his usually calm voice. "Your posture is particularly important during this exercise."

Finally, I snapped. "Look, if I could keep my back straight, I wouldn't be having so many problems with it." I let go of the overhead bar, and it swayed above me in a dangerous arch. "I'm trying, but it hurts to do this, okay?"

He grasped ahold of the bar and steadied it. "Okay, I'm sorry. I was pushing." He exhaled. "Let's see if we can try something else that might still work that same muscle group."

He came up with an exercise—"lateral presses" or some such thing—where I was pushing only against his hands instead. And, while it was easier to maintain correct posture now, it was hell on my concentration.

Chance had a clean but masculine scent, like he'd just showered in some kind of pheromone musk.

His hands were warm and rough and strong and sensual. All at once. It took no imagination whatsoever to picture what he could do with those long fingers.

And don't get me started on his lips. He wasn't quick to smile, but when he did, his mouth looked so kissable that I could barely breathe for wanting to press my lips against his.

So, I tried to focus on everything in the gym but him. It wasn't working.

"You seem distracted today," he observed from above me, a puzzled look crossing his handsome, chiseled face.

You're a regular Sherlock, I wanted to say. But I didn't.

I'd read half of that pink relationship book in the past two days, though, and I knew my attraction to Chance must just be a reaction against the serious step of introducing Grant to my family. So, I exhaled slowly, forced myself to meet Chance's eye, and said, "Sorry. I just have a lot on my mind today."

"Because of your big date tonight?" he guessed.

I nodded. "If I can last long enough to make it to Bangkok Gardens at seven-thirty, I'll be good. But until then..." I sighed. "I have a loving but very involved family. I get nervous about introducing anyone to my parents for the first time."

He didn't say anything, but a glint of some emotion flashed in his eyes and the brackets around those kissable lips of his tightened.

"What?" I asked.

It was rare to see a crack in his estimable control but, for a second, his golden eyes betrayed him, revealing an array of feelings. And this time I could identify what a few of them were: Sadness. Compassion. Wistfulness. Pain. One following the other, like cascading dominoes.

"I—um... I'm a little jealous," he said, which wasn't

one of the emotions I thought I'd recognized. "I wish I could do what you're doing. Bring someone home to meet my parents. They both died too young, so..." He shrugged.

"Oh, Chance, I'm so sorry," I whispered.

He smiled at me, a devastating smile that pierced my soul with its beauty and its heartbreak. "It's okay. It's been a while since it happened," he said, and I remembered that it had been over five years since Mrs. Michaelsen had died unexpectedly from a stroke. I could recall my parents talking about it. They'd said her husband had passed away just a couple of years before that, too. Stomach cancer.

"I'm sure the sadness never leaves you," I said.

"It doesn't," he admitted, "but they gave us all a lot of good memories while they were alive." He paused. "So, I hope everything goes well for you tonight. Enjoy having a reason to be nervous."

Never had I wanted to throw my arms around someone more, and not just so I could kiss him. I wanted to hug Chance Michaelsen. Hug the young man he was seven years ago when his dad died. If he was twenty-eight now—just two years older than me—he would have been only twenty-one then. Barely a man. And then, at twenty-three, to have lost his mother, too.

I wondered for the first time how much his parents' early deaths must have impacted him. Wondered if this was part of his reason for becoming such a health fanatic. Was he trying to outwit the Grim Reaper and earn himself a few extra years of old age? If so, I couldn't blame him.

His words—"enjoy having a reason to be nervous"—stayed with me for the rest of the day, though. His perspective was one I hadn't expected, and I played over and over again the various shades of meaning inherent in that phrase.

I went back home to shower and get ready for the evening ahead. Until very recently, I'd considered only the practical advantages of still living with my parents. Aside from the traditional and cultural aspect of staying there, working with them at The Gala made it convenient and economical. But, maybe, too much togetherness wasn't always a good thing, eh?

"Hey, I need to get in the bathroom sometime this century," my brother Dimitri called out, banging on the door a couple of times like he used to when we were in high school. He was a year and a half older than me (and, yes, he also still lived at home) but, in my opinion, he acted like a teenager most of the time.

"I've only been in here ten minutes," I called back, irritated. "I'm sure you can find something useful to do for ten minutes more so I can dry my hair."

I heard only grumbling and a few curse words on the other side of the bathroom door, but I knew better than to let Dimitri come in until after I was completely done. He hogged the mirror, messed up the countertop with blobs of hair gel, and primped and preened like a sixteen-year-old girl before prom. I was the one with the big date tonight, not him. I needed space.

I'd just finished blow drying when my brother pounded on the door again. "Better hurry up, Nia, your cell phone is going crazy."

Oh, no. Was Grant cancelling?

I opened the door and Dimitri pushed his way in. I grabbed my hairbrush and left to check my phone. No voicemails or texts from Grant. Whew. But there were several missed calls from Donna.

I called her back. "Hi, what's up?" I asked.

"Just checking in with you," she said, slightly out of breath as usual. The ambient sounds in the background struck me as familiar, though. Was she calling from Harbor Fitness?

"Are you at the gym?" I asked.

"Yep. On the elliptical," Donna said, puffing. "Just saw Mr. Stonyface wandering around the place and thought of you. How's the training with him going?"

It had been a while since I'd thought of Chance as anything but a hot-blooded American male, despite his cool, sculpted appearance. His facial expressions were more subtle than most, but his eyes were rather eloquent if you looked carefully enough. I elected not to mention this revelation to Donna, however.

"Fine," I said. "My back is slowly improving, and he's got me doing a bunch of exercises to strengthen my abdom—"

"Oh, good," she said, cutting me off. "As long as the prick is doing his job. Didn't I tell you that he was totally focused on fitness? He probably doesn't even realize you're a living, breathing woman." She laughed.

"Um—" I began, but then I stopped. I didn't know how to defend Chance without simultaneously insulting Donna and her lack of perception. As much as I wished I could deny it, I was envious that she'd gotten to kiss him. Maybe even sleep with him. (Oh, boy...what must that have been like?!) But it didn't seem as though she'd gotten to *know* him very well, and I didn't appreciate the things she said about him now. It felt as if we were talking about two different men. One of us must have misread Chance. And maybe I was deceiving myself, but I didn't think it was me. "How long did you two date again?" I asked.

"Less than a month. Why?" she replied, her voice suspicious. "Did he say anything about me?"

"No, no," I said quickly. "Not even once. I was just curious."

"Not even once? Hmm."

There was an awkward pause, and I realized my mistake. For some reason, Donna must still be emotionally invested in the relationship. She didn't necessarily *like* Chance, but there was a part of her that still wanted him to like *her*.

"I just meant that he never gossiped about you, Donna."

"Well, that's good," she said. Then, "Did he make a pass at you or something?"

"Oh, no." She didn't need to know about our flirting. Or my sexual fantasies about the guy. For all I knew, they could be completely one-sided daydreams anyway. My intuition told me otherwise, though. "I actually have a date with someone else tonight, so I'd better get ready for—"

"Who?"

I winced. She was probably going to keep me on the phone for another hour once she heard the name. "Grant Jordan."

"The plastics CEO? Oh. My. Gawd. Nia! You're so lucky," she gushed. "How did you meet him? Tell me everything!"

I didn't have time for "everything," but I gave her the highlights. How one of the Jordan-Luccio Corporation execs was Greek and his parents were friends with my parents. That the exec had gotten The Gala a catering gig at the office. I went downtown one Thursday morning to bring them some samples for tasting and to finalize the agreement, and Grant was there. He claimed to love the samples. (A sure way to win over a Greek girl's heart.) And the moment the two of us were alone in the conference room, Grant had asked me out on the spot for the following evening.

"Yes, I'd like that," I'd said to him.

He'd winked and replied, "Good. In that case, I'll double the order. One for the office, and one for a party at my house next weekend. Maybe, if you enjoy our date tomorrow, you can join me at that gathering, too."

That was a couple of months ago, and we'd been going out almost every weekend since then.

Donna sighed heavily on the line. "I'm so jealous! How come I never meet rich and sexy men like that? I only find duds like Chance Michaelsen."

I swallowed back my anger at her words. She'd

misunderstood and misrepresented Chance, and I knew it, but I didn't have time to argue with her or listen to her self-pitying refrains about never finding a good man. It just got old. Sometimes I sensed that Donna was stuck in that same immature teen-girl phase from high school. Eight years ago, that was annoying but age-appropriate. Now, it was a lot of the former and none of the latter.

When I finally was able to hang up, I jumped into high gear. Grant was going to be at The Gala in just thirty-five minutes! I had to get dressed, put on makeup, do at least a decade's worth of Zen meditation... Good thing I didn't have a long commute.

"Not bad," Dimitri said, eyeing my outfit, once I came downstairs. Our family home was connected to the restaurant, which was extremely convenient for events like this.

"Thanks, I think," I said to my brother.

"So, am I gonna like this hotshot business guy of yours?" he asked.

"I don't care whether you like him or not," I lied. "But you'd better be very polite to him."

Dimitri rolled his eyes. "As long as he treats you well, Nia." Then he shot me a warm and genuine grin. "Don't worry about me. I'll behave." He lowered his voice. "I make no promises for Mama and Papa, though. And you know Aunt Helen..."

We both laughed. Aunt Helen was on the talkative side, and she usually just blurted the first thing that popped into her carefully coiffed head. She was my mom's older sister and the mother of my Wisconsin cousins, Nick and Jason. Nick, the younger of the two, was the one who now worked at The Playbook, a fancy sports-themed restaurant in Chicago, so I saw him there every once in a while. In fact, that was where Grant and I had gone for our third date.

Tonight, though, we had seven-thirty reservations at one of the nicest and quietest restaurants in Mirabelle

Harbor—my favorite Thai place, Bangkok Gardens. I figured that would give Grant and me an excuse to leave the family inquisition at The Gala after no more than forty-five minutes of questioning. If my level of anxiety was any indication, that was about forty minutes too long.

Enjoy having a reason to be nervous.

I thought about Chance's words again. He was right. I needed to enjoy tonight. This was a happy occasion, getting to introduce my family to a guy I liked. Maybe even the man I'd marry. I was lucky I could share this with my parents, my brother, and my other relatives. I knew they were going to keep loving me no matter what happened, so I just had to relax. Go with the flow.

Aunt Helen and Uncle Theo were sitting with my parents at a large circular table. My cousin Jason had stayed up in Wisconsin to tend to the business, but his brother Nick drove up to see us all. He and Dimitri were talking sports, my dad and my uncle were talking politics, and my mom and her sister were talking recipes...when Grant Jordan walked into The Gala.

He was dressed like he'd just stepped out of a men's clothing catalog—an expensive one. Dark Italian suit. Red silk tie. Leather shoes so polished that they gleamed. He grinned at me from across the room, and my aunt whispered some kind of Greek blessing under her breath.

"Hi, Nia," he said, his eyes sweeping the restaurant and taking in the collection of relatives. "I've been looking forward to meeting everyone."

Aunt Helen murmured another prayer, something that evoked the spirit of the blessed Virgin Mary and requested a forthcoming marriage and a multitude of children.

My mother just nodded.

"Grant," I said, "I'm so glad you could stop by. Let me introduce you to my family."

As I went around the table, one by one, and made the official introductions, Grant looked so completely in his element that I had to remind myself that he wasn't Greek. He easily slipped into the conversation the men were having about new international trade laws and the state of the euro, but when my mother brought out the *mezethes*— the hot and cold appetizers, including a platter of *triopita* triangles, *spanakopita* squares, skillet-fried *saganaki* cheese, *dolmades*, and some olives, cucumbers, and sliced tomatoes—Grant gratefully accepted a bit of everything. He made a show of enjoying every bite, and praised my mom's handiwork until she blushed. He was impressively good at this.

Nick, who was openly gay and in a happy partnership, had met Grant once before at The Playbook. My cousin gave me an enthusiastic thumbs up behind Grant's back, while Dimitri just raised his eyebrows and grinned. "He's in," he whispered in my ear before Grant and I left on our dinner date.

And my brother was right. Even our father, who could be less than welcoming of "outsiders," was slapping Grant on the back and offering him "just a little ouzo" before we walked out the door.

Grant seemed pleased to oblige. "Good thing Nia and I can walk to Bangkok Gardens from here," he said to my delighted relatives, as he downed his second small glass of the licorice-flavored alcohol.

"Opa!" Uncle Theo said.

"Opa!" everyone else chorused.

Yeah. At this rate, it was probably going to be a couple of hours before it would be safe for Grant to drive anywhere.

He held my hand as we left my parents' restaurant, knowing we were being observed by my family. "How'd I do?" he murmured, once we were halfway down Main Street.

"You were brilliant," I had to admit. "They loved you."

"Good." There was pride in his voice, and I was

grateful for the respectful way he'd interacted with my relatives, but as soon as we were out of sight from The Gala, he let go of my hand and reached for his phone.

"I just need to check for messages real quick," he told me.

So, when we turned onto Crescent Lane, where the Thai place was located, even though it had only been a few minutes since we left The Gala, I already felt weirdly disconnected from him. Like the stage show part of the evening was over, and now it was back to business. Literally. He answered three texts and responded to one voicemail before we even reached the front doors of the restaurant.

I would have been more impressed with his multitasking ability if it didn't seem to be in such sharp contrast to his incredibly attentive behavior when he was with my family. In retrospect, it cast a weirdly superficial light on that whole interaction.

But he smiled winningly when we got to Bangkok Gardens, and he opened the door for me. It was a nice spring evening, but it was always a little nippy by the lake in April, and tonight was no exception. I was glad to be inside.

"Hello, Nia," a very recognizable voice in the lobby said to me.

"Chance?" He was sitting on one of the benches, not nearly as surprised to see me as I was to see him. He was dressed casually, but not in his fitness-instructor clothing for a change. He had on fitted blue jeans and a nice long-sleeved jersey. Maroon-colored and very silky. I realized I'd never seen him in anything but workout shirts, shorts, or sweats before. "What are you doing here?" I asked.

He eyed Grant with undisguised curiosity, but then turned his gaze on me. "It's my favorite carryout place. They've got great spring rolls. Very healthy," he added with a grin.

Grant, who had been scrolling through his texts again, finally put away his phone and glanced at me expectantly. Ah. I supposed a formal introduction was in order.

"Grant, this is my personal trainer, Chance Michaelsen. Chance, this is my...um, this is Grant Jordan."

"I'm her boyfriend," Grant filled in for me, which was the first time he'd used the term in public. It denoted a kind of relationship exclusivity that I wasn't sure he'd felt until now. I glanced at him with interest as he reached out to shake Chance's hand, full of his usual confidence.

Chance stood up to grasp it, which was when I realized that Chance was actually a couple of inches taller than Grant and, also, significantly more muscular. In the cavernous gym, Chance was completely in his element and seemed less imposing somehow, surrounded by all of those big pieces of exercise equipment and dwarfed, as we all were there, by the high ceilings. His physicality didn't stand out quite so much at Harbor Fitness. In the compact lobby of a Thai restaurant, however, it did.

I saw Grant blink in surprise.

The two men sized each other up, and I caught an expression on Chance's face that was different from any other look I'd witnessed on him before. It was like he'd just issued a challenge that he knew the illustrious Grant Jordan wouldn't be able to refuse.

"Nice to meet you, Chance," Grant said with the faux sincerity of a newscaster covering a natural disaster.

"Likewise, Grant," Chance said with reciprocal sincerity and deliberate precision. The politeness between them was so forced I almost laughed aloud.

"Your order is ready," one of the male servers informed my personal trainer, coming out from the kitchen and holding up a neatly packaged carryout bag.

Chance thanked the guy just as the hostess approached Grant and me, asking if we had a reservation.

Grant stepped forward to give our names while Chance

moved closer to me.

"How'd it go with your family?" he whispered.

"Good," I whispered back.

He looked like he didn't quite believe me.

"No, it was fine. Really," I said. "Only a little weird," I admitted, almost under my breath.

But I knew Chance heard me.

"They're ready for us, beautiful," Grant said loudly to me.

"All right," I said.

Chance nodded at Grant, then at me. "Have a nice evening." Then, just to me, he added, "See you Monday, Nia."

"Okay," I murmured as Grant and the hostess led me away from him and to our table. I stole one quick look over my shoulder just as Chance was striding out the door with his carryout spring rolls. He looked back at me at the same time. That electrifying sizzle zipped between us once again. Then he was gone.

Grant and I were seated at our table, handed menus, and left on our own for a few minutes.

He asked me a few questions about what my favorite entrées and appetizers were (cashew chicken, massaman curry, shrimp satays...) and added a few of his own before ordering a mini feast for us.

I agreed to everything he suggested.

"Hey, I'm leaning toward the pad thai—beef or, maybe, pork. What do you think?"

"Either sounds good," I said.

"What about splitting an order of spring rolls?"

"Sure."

I realized now that it had been much the same way at the other restaurants we'd dined at together. Grant always took the lead. Always made a splashy show out of getting us a collection of interesting dishes to try. Always turned the date into a "happening."

I'd never complained about it, and it would be disingenuous to do that—he had been trying to make every event more fun, more memorable, somewhat larger than life—but I was aware that this might also be a distancing device. While it gave the appearance to the outside world that Grant and I were doing things together, we weren't really getting to know each other deeply. We were chatting, but we weren't conversing.

And although we'd been going out for a couple of months, we'd been on just seven or eight actual dates. Given Grant's work schedule, we only managed to get together once during each weekend. Certainly some people expected that we knew each other better by now. That we were sleeping together. But we weren't even close to a step like that. We'd kissed at the end of every date and it was really nice, but he wasn't pushing for more than that. For the first time, I wondered, *Why?*

"So, it looks like it was a busy week," I observed. "Any particularly big projects going on?"

Grant looked up guiltily from his phone, which he'd been sneaking looks at whenever he thought my attention was elsewhere.

"Nia, yeah. Please forgive me for not being totally with it tonight." He reached across the table and placed his hand over mine. It wasn't as large or as warm as Chance's hand, but I liked Grant's touch. It was gentle without being at all effeminate. "There's a merger in progress, and it has me kind of distracted."

"That's okay," I said. "I understand. Can you talk about the merger or the different projects you have going on? I'd like to understand more about what you do."

He smiled at me. "The merger, no. I can't say anything about that until it's been finalized. But I do have a new charity project I can share with you. It's the Lake Geneva Fund."

He talked about that at length. Grant was a dedicated

supporter of several good causes like this one—a rehabilitation center for children who'd sustained serious injuries in accidents. And I listened.

But even though I'd asked the question, my mind had a hard time staying on the topic. Just like when I was at the bookstore. Even when I was trying to focus on Grant, my brain would start fixating on Chance instead.

On things like the way Chance didn't *talk* about any charity work he might be doing, he just *did* it. If he saw someone in need—the young widow by the grocery store, Julia Crane, or the older gentleman at the gym, Mr. Alleghany—Chance would just jump in and help them.

And my personal trainer's appearance at the Thai restaurant was, I knew, not remotely coincidental. I'd told him the exact time we'd be here, never dreaming that he'd show up under any pretext at all. As quiet as Chance could be, he seemed to be giving me a signal that was loud, direct, and very clear: *I've got my eyes on you.*

Grant was still talking about his company and other work-related things when my phone buzzed, alerting me to a new text.

My initial reaction was one of annoyance. I'd had enough of Grant's phone calls, texts, and messages. I didn't need the people in *my* life interrupting us, too.

I didn't recognize the phone number, but was stunned to see Chance's name once I clicked to read the text.

Hey, Nia. Glad to see you at the restaurant. In the event that you need an early out tonight, just let me know. I can call you with an "urgent" message, if a getaway excuse is desired. ~Chance

Holy moly. What was this?

I immediately reached for my wine and drank about half the glass.

Grant was looking at me strangely. "Everything okay?"

I nodded. "Just thirsty. And, um, this riesling is excellent."

He smiled. Grant prided himself on his knowledge of wines. "Glad you like it." And then he launched into a new story about the Jordan-Luccio Corporation and some plans that he and his business partner Patrick had to expand the company to London.

I pretended to listen, but my head was reeling. How had Chance gotten my cell number?

Then, answering my own question, I remembered I'd written it on my initial sign-up form. The one I'd filled out before my first training session at Harbor Fitness.

However, that meant Chance had either written it down during the past week or he'd returned to the gym to look it up. Some work had gone into getting ahold of it, in any case, and his text to me wasn't a spontaneous, casual act. Maybe I was imagining things, but Chance didn't give off an air of recklessness. I got the sense that he didn't do anything that wasn't carefully planned, well considered, premeditated.

Which was why this sort of freaked me out.

Chance Michaelsen wasn't just flirting with me over fitness equipment anymore. He seemed to be suggesting that he was available. Now. If I wanted to ditch Grant.

Or, maybe, he just thought he was being helpful to a...friend or client or fellow Mirabelle Harbor citizen or something. Could that be?

When Grant got yet another phone call five minutes later and excused himself to answer it in the lobby, I took this opportunity to respond to Chance's mystifying text:

Thanks for asking, Chance. That's very thoughtful of you, but I'm okay for now. Hope you're having fun evening, too.

I sent it but then wondered if, perhaps, it sounded a bit too dismissive, especially if he thought he was just being helpful. I decided to add this post script:

So, what are you doing tonight?

Grant came back to the table and, for the longest time,

there was no reply from Chance. I was still mulling over his text in my mind. Pondering the reason for it. I mean, I appreciated the option he'd given me, but I was puzzled by the offer. What made Chance, after just a brief meeting with Grant, think I needed rescuing from my handsome and successful businessman boyfriend?

Maybe I was a little bored tonight, sure, but I was perfectly safe. And it wasn't as though my friends and family didn't know where I was and who I was with.

Grant and I were just getting ready to order coffee and dessert when my phone buzzed with Chance's reply. It came in list form, and I smothered a gasp of surprise when I snuck a glance at it:

1. Eating spring rolls.

2. Watching either a baseball game...or My Big Fat Greek Wedding. *(The Cubs are losing. Might learn something more interesting from the movie.)*

3. Thinking of you.

Well, alrighty then. Nothing subtle about that, eh, Chance?

CHAPTER SIX

~*Chance*~

One of the shitty downsides of being so attuned to your own body and familiar with things like your resting heart rate was that, when there was the slightest change in your respiratory, circulatory, muscular, or nervous systems, you were immediately aware of it.

When Nia Pappayiannis walked into Harbor Fitness on Monday afternoon, my pulse suddenly kicked it up to the level of a decent jog. I could feel the blood pumping through my arteries like crazy, even though I was standing still. Every muscle in my body tensed. And my neurotransmitters were having a field day sending signals to receptors in my brain. All of them seemed to be shouting, "Look at her!"

And I was looking. And feeling. I couldn't remember having a physiological reaction like this in years. Not since I danced with cute Claudia Mazur at prom more than a decade ago. I'd had such an intense crush on her.

But this thing with Nia was even more intense. And I sure as hell wasn't seventeen anymore.

When she waved at me from across the gym, just knowing I was going to get to stand near her, be engulfed in her soft scent, maybe get to touch a few parts of her—her shoulders, her back, her hands—made me uncomfortably aware of how my blood pressure was skyrocketing.

"Hey, Chance," Nia said, slightly out of breath as she reached me near the free weights. She warily eyed the three-pound hand weights I was holding. "Are we doing that swan thing again?"

"The swan dive," I said. "And, yes."

She wrinkled her nose. "Hmm."

"And the reverse fly, too, which I know is your favorite." She *hated* the reverse fly.

"Ugh," she said, grimacing.

I almost laughed. She was adorable.

But we immediately got to work on her strengthening routine, and she did all of the reps and sets I told her to do without further complaint.

If this had been any other session, any day before seeing her and that boyfriend of hers on Friday night, I would have been pleased by our easy rapport. But it wasn't. And I wasn't.

She didn't look a fraction as nervous as I felt. Not remotely as affected by me as I was by her. She didn't behave toward me like I thought she would, especially after my last text on Friday when I said I was thinking about her.

No.

She looked at me as if I hadn't said anything at all.

So, maybe she hadn't gotten that text. Or she thought I didn't mean it. Or she was hoping I didn't. No matter which way it fell, I didn't like it.

Michael Jackson's "Human Nature" started to play on LOVE FM, and I was sorely tempted to call out to Gillian at the front desk to turn off the radio. I'd have some words with my brother about his damn playlist later.

Just when I was starting to think that any attraction that Nia and I had between us was all in my head, we did the hand press exercise again.

For the first time since she came into the gym today, I got the sense that she was finally noticing me. That she was aware of my skin touching her skin. My breath mingling with her breath. She kept staring at me with those huge dark eyes of hers, but then looking away. It was all I could do not to trail a row of kisses down her cheek, along the side of her neck, across her shoulders, and then lower.

I swallowed and heard her take a shaky breath, but she still said nothing. Finished her exercises without a sound. Gave me no encouragement. No sign that my wanting her was welcome.

Why not? Did she really like that poser Grant Jordan? Or worse, did she *love* him? Just the thought of him touching her—*in bed with her!*—made me kind of nuts.

"It's 2:34," she said, watching me as I set up one last exercise, this time using the pull-down bar on a lat machine. It would bring us face to face for two sets of ten reps.

"So?"

"So, my half hour is up."

I shrugged. "I don't have another client until three o'clock today." I motioned for her to sit down and reach upward toward the bar. Anger and wanting mixed together, and I just had the overwhelming urge to test her somehow. Make her pay attention to me. Get her to show her cards to me the way I had to her.

"What if I need to leave?" she asked.

"Do you?"

She gazed at me for a long moment, probably trying to formulate some sort of an argument. But, in the end, she only said, "I guess not."

I considered it a weird kind of triumph.

We'd done this exercise only once before. She had to

pull down on the bar and I'd provide extra resistance, facing her and holding it steady. It had been an uncomfortable one for her when we'd tried it previously, but she'd gotten stronger over the past several sessions. I knew she could handle it now.

We'd barely done six reps of the first set when the Berlin song "Take My Breath Away" came on.

I heard her laugh lightly and, when she reached the tenth rep, she stopped and shook her head. "I think one set is going to do it, Chance."

She let go of the bar, abruptly stood up, and took several steps away from me, like I was a walking contagion.

"Gotta run," she whispered. "See you on Wednesday, though." And then she bolted out of the building.

I wiped down the equipment, put the hand weights back on the rack and then, when I was sure no one would connect what I was doing with what I was feeling, I went a couple of rounds—just me against the punching bag—until my three o'clock client walked in the door.

❀❀❀

The next day, when I was positive I had a little more control, I called Blake and told him we were going out for lunch.

"I'll drive. Pick you up in fifteen minutes," I informed him. I didn't leave him any choice in the matter.

He seemed a little surprised by the demand, but I knew his work schedule and he couldn't argue. He had an hour before he needed to get to the radio station. And any idle time Blake had on his hands might as well be the devil's playground.

"So, what's on your mind, little brother?" he asked me when we'd gotten our deli sandwiches and were seated on our favorite rock by the lake. We'd come here as a family when our parents were still alive. A part of me could still feel their presence.

"I can't talk to Derek about this because, once he met Olivia, it was like he'd never dated anyone else in his life. Chandler is wandering around somewhere in the southeastern United States and is lost until he wants to be found. And Sharlene is a girl."

Blake laughed. "So, I'm Option D. Last one left, right?"

"Pretty much." I grinned at him. "Actually, I think you're the only one who might be able to help me anyway. There's this woman—"

"There always is."

"Yeah, well, I'm kind of crazy about her, and I think—I *think*—she's noticing me, too, but I'm not positive. I don't know. This is just not normal for me. I'm not used to feeling this...insecure or whatever. This unsure of someone's feelings. I send out these obvious signals to her and I think she's sending signals back, but there's been nothing definite."

Blake took a big bite of his sandwich and stared at me thoughtfully as he chewed. Finally, he said, "You mean, she's not actually throwing herself at you, like most women?"

"Right," I had to admit. That was the usual scenario, and Nia definitely hadn't done that.

My brother rolled his eyes. "Did you maybe try asking her out?"

I shook my head. "No. There's a complication—"

"There always is."

"Yeah, well, it involves another guy."

"Oh, shit."

"Her supposed 'boyfriend,' I guess."

"You *guess* that she has a boyfriend? Are you kidding me, Chance? You're encroaching on another guy's girl?"

"I don't think it's a serious thing. There's no real

commitment, from what I can tell. She just introduced him to her parents for the first time on Friday and—"

"She introduced him to the family? Bro, that's kind of serious."

I shook my head. "But I saw them together Friday night, and that wasn't the vibe I got. Not at all. He was barely looking at her. And she seemed...not entirely herself. Thing is, he's a big shot. One of the dudes at the Jordan-Luccio Corporation."

"Which one of the dudes? A manager or something?"

"No. The Jordan one."

Blake raised a dark eyebrow, impressed. "You're telling me that you're trying to steal Grant Jordan's girlfriend?"

"Screw you. I'm not trying to *steal* her. I think she's attracted to me, too, but she just won't say anything. So, then I find myself wondering... Oh, never mind."

"What?"

I kicked at a pebble with my sneaker. "Maybe she's not saying anything because she *wants* Grant Jordan."

"Do you mean his body? Or do you mean his money, his position in society, and his relative fame?"

"All of the above," I admitted. "I suppose he's not ugly. Women seemed to find him attractive, anyway." I shrugged. "And I know his net worth is in the millions, but I don't get the sense that she's a gold digger. I just wonder if, maybe, he's the better man."

Blake squinted at me and put down his sandwich. "Look, Chance, I'm your brother. I'm biased. But I don't think a woman could find a better man than you."

"I'm not fishing for complimen—"

"I know you're not. Hear me out, though. All bias aside, you're not asking the right question here. It's not whether Grant is a better man, which I think is debatable and highly unlikely." Blake looked me in the eye and, without the slightest trace of humor, said, "The question is whether Grant is the better man *for her*."

I sighed. He was right. Too often others underestimated my brother or dismissed his opinion because he was a hothead. But Blake could be more perceptive than many people—including our own siblings—realized.

"What if she doesn't know who's better for her yet?" I asked.

"Give her a little time. Watch her reactions. Maybe try to ask her a few more questions to get at her true feelings. Is she someone you see fairly often?"

"Yeah. She's one of my personal training clients."

"When does she come in?"

"Monday, Wednesday, and Friday afternoons from two to two-thirty. Which reminds me, if you could please knock off the really suggestive love songs during that particular half hour, I'd appreciate it. No more freakin' 'Sexual Healing,' got it?"

Blake threw his head back and laughed. "Oh, I got it all right. I'll see what I can do."

✿❋✿

Wednesday afternoon took about three and a half years to finally get here, but I was determined to put my brother's advice to good use.

I'd watch Nia.

I'd try to ask a few questions to get at her true feelings about Grant Jordan.

And I'd let her know—in subtle and not-so-subtle ways—that I was interested in her. Very, very interested. But if she wanted me, she'd have to make the first move.

So, when she showed up at two p.m., I smiled at her. Asked her how her day was going.

"Um, fine," she said, her tone somewhat guarded. "Why?"

"Relax, Nia. I just want to know how you are."

She shot me a look that said she thought I was up to something. Which, let's face it, I was. I just smiled at her again, even bigger this time.

I pointed toward the mats. "Torso twists to start."

She rolled her eyes, but she walked with me to that open section and grabbed the weights. She was using the five-pound ones for this exercise now. Progress! Another thing that had improved was her overall posture. She was holding herself taller and straighter while doing the exercises. I was impressed, and I told her so.

She blushed a little. It was so damned cute. "I've been trying to remember," she murmured. I could tell she was pleased I'd taken the time to say something about it, though.

She did three sets of twenty reps, and then I introduced a new core crunch—perfect for ab strengthening—that used a mid-sized exercise ball.

One of the advantages-slash-disadvantages of working so closely with clients was that I got to know their position quirks fairly quickly. Nia had a tendency to drop her right shoulder and slouch to that side unless specifically instructed to pull herself back. So, for each brand-new exercise, I'd have to help her get into the correct position, at least initially. And this involved touching her shoulder and physically placing it where it needed to be.

It was my favorite part of my sessions with Nia.

As I knelt behind her on the mat and helped position her upper body for the crunches, I could feel the tightening of her biceps. The extra strength they were beginning to develop, even in the short time frame that we'd been working together.

Nia had a naturally lithe and graceful form when she moved her arms, like a dancer. But the swell of her breasts and the curve of her hips continued to make my mouth run dry. These workout sessions weren't going to change her shape, nor would I have wanted them to, but I thought they were beginning to make her more confident about her body. More knowledgeable about the way it moved.

I didn't think she'd be caught unaware for as long now if she suddenly found herself in an uncomfortable position. Her muscle memory would kick in and remind her to hold herself with a more correct, pain-free posture. She always seemed vaguely surprised by the relief she felt in her spine and the muscles surrounding it when she pulled her shoulders back and her chest popped outward. At the same time, she also looked a little embarrassed by it. As if she was worried about her breasts being too much on display.

"Don't be self conscious, Nia," I told her. "You're using absolutely correct form here. I wish everyone had lines this perfect." I motioned at the angle of her torso to the floor. It was a beautiful forty-five degrees.

She laughed. "You're insane," she said, but she held the position and began doing her first set of crunches with the ball.

About halfway through, my brother's voice came on the air. The usual radio station identification thing he always did. Then Blake said, "This next song is for a guy who asked me yesterday if he should pursue a girl he's fallen for. I say, go for it, man."

The tune that came on was by the duo Evan and Jaron. A love song called "Crazy for This Girl."

I groaned. *I'm gonna kill him.*

"What?" Nia asked, puffing with exertion.

Crap. I didn't say that aloud, did I?

"Nothing, nothing. One more set," I told her, trying to keep the wanting out of my voice, but she probably still heard it.

She sent me an odd look that didn't seem to have anything to do with the exercise.

"Just a few more reps to go," I said, trying to get her to refocus on the crunches. Once she reached number six, I added, "You're almost there. Seven, eight, nine—"

"Whoa, just look at you two," a shrill voice said from behind me, drowning out my count of ten.

Donna. Aw, hell.

"Hey," Nia said to her friend. "What a surprise to see you here." The two women smiled at each other, but I couldn't tell how genuine it was on either side. There seemed to be friction of some kind. Huh.

Donna appraised the two of us on the mat with a look that was equal parts suspicious, curious, and accusatory. "Must take a lot of training and skill to count all the way up to ten like that. Right, Chance?" she said, playing off the insult to me as if it were a joke.

But I knew it wasn't.

Donna liked to insinuate that I was a dumb jock whenever possible. I'd broken up with her and, therefore, must be utterly lacking in sense. Truth was, I knew she had a very fragile ego, and I'd already bruised it. Badly.

I'd take the heat for that and not fight back, though. Long ago, I made it a rule never to pick on people who were weaker than me in any area, so I was just going to let her get her digs in. I could ignore her and, besides, I didn't want her to make a scene.

Nia, however, took a totally different tack.

She shot Donna a steely look. "You're so right. It *does* take skill," she agreed. "Chance has an instinctive ability to know just how long each rep should be for optimal results." She set the exercise ball firmly on the mat and stood up to her full height. Shoulders back. Chest out. Perfect posture. Her expression was that of a fierce lady warrior. I saw Donna take a surprised step backward.

I stood up as well, too stunned and pleased by the unexpected defense to say anything. I didn't need anybody to bolster my ego, but I couldn't believe how grateful I was to know that Nia cared enough to *want* to defend me.

Much as I hated showy public displays of affection or

sappy outpourings of emotion, I could have kissed her right then and there in the middle of Harbor Fitness. My sister would probably take me in for a psych evaluation if she knew what was running through my mind, but that was how much Nia's words meant to me.

"And you know what else?" Nia said brightly to her friend, adding a piercing smile. "My back is feeling *so* much better. Even after just five sessions. Chance is a rare find." She nodded solemnly in my direction. "He knew exactly which exercises would help. I'm very thankful to *you,* Donna, for recommending him so highly to me."

Well, that shut my ex up for good. She sputtered something unintelligible at us—"Have fun," maybe?—and backed even further away.

"Good seeing you, Donna," I managed, trying to ease the sting of her shock but hardly able to keep from laughing. In all the months I'd known that woman, I couldn't remember ever seeing her so close to speechless.

I caught Nia's smile as her friend skulked away from us, but then she masked it. "Don't get a big head or anything, Chance, but everything I said was true."

Did she know what she was doing to me?

Did she have a clue how much I admired her? Enjoyed being with her? Wanted her?

I couldn't tell her any of this, I knew, but I tried to pour what I was feeling into my gaze, hoping she might just see it in my eyes. "Thank you, Nia." I paused. "And I promise not to get too big of a big head."

For a long moment, we just stared at each other. Wordless, but I felt as though a whole conversation could be packed into that silence.

Then her lips twisted slightly and she said, "So, Friday, I can't come in."

"Why?"

She exhaled. "I have a, um, prior engagement."

My heart skipped a few beats at the word

"engagement," even though I knew better. Knew it wasn't a precursor to a wedding. At least not yet.

But, suddenly, it seemed imperative to make sure our workout sessions were more of a priority for her. We were halfway through them already, and I was running out of time to win her over.

So, I took an unhappy guess and asked, "Another date with Grant Jordan?"

She nodded, but it wasn't an enthusiastic nod. *Good.* Although she looked worried about something, which, in turn, worried me.

"Well, you have my cell number if your plans change. Just text me and let me know," I said, sending her a significant look. "I'm free Friday afternoon and evening, and I can fit you in almost any time that night. So, even if you come home late, I can meet you here. The gym is open until midnight."

"That—that won't be necessary, Chance. You don't need to be quite so accommodating of my schedule."

"It's no trouble at all," I assured her. "You've made such tremendous progress already, I don't want you to backslide or reinjure yourself."

She looked amused. "I've never known anyone who's shown this level of concern for my health and wellness."

I smiled. "What can I say, Nia? I care."

She grinned just as the Goo Goo Dolls started singing "Let Love In." I watched her pause and listen to the first verse—eyes on me, ears tuned in to 102.5 LOVE FM. "I like this song," she declared when the chorus started.

I nodded. I did, too.

So, maybe I wouldn't kill Blake...yet.

She flashed one more smile at me. God, what I wouldn't give to know what she was thinking... And then she skipped away to the beat of the music.

CHAPTER SEVEN

~*Nia*~

Chance Michaelsen was going to be the death of me.

Or at least my unrelenting attraction to him could very well mean the end of my perfectly envisioned future and my currently harmonious relationship with my mother.

"When will we see your young man again?" Mama inquired on Thursday. "That handsome Grant Jordan?"

"Tomorrow afternoon," I told her.

"Oh, good!" she squealed and actually clapped her hands. "I liked him."

"I know."

"He was so polite when he came to visit. Attractive. Successful. Had good taste. Did you hear what he said about my *triopita* triangles?"

"Yes, Mama. I heard."

"They were 'delectable,' he said. And he ate three of them," she added proudly. "And he still tried the *spanakopita* and the *saganaki* and the *dolmades*—"

"Grant has excellent taste," I reiterated, "and a very hearty appetite."

"I predict you will marry him, Antonia," my mother informed me. "And your Aunt Helen thinks so, too."

Oh, no. There was nothing quite so damning as a marital prediction from Aunt Helen. If she guessed right, she'd gloat for decades. Literally. If she guessed wrong, she'd spend years pointing out the flaws in the couple's relationship.

My mother and I were making a few large trays of our signature *galaktoboureko*, but as soon as the dessert pastry was ready to be popped into The Gala's industrial-sized ovens, I escaped the kitchen for a while and stole upstairs to read my pink book.

Just one chapter left to go, and it was on "relationship testing."

The author wrote:

> *"Once we leave school, no one likes to think that our behavior is being watched, assessed, and scored according to any kind of a rubric, but it is. Dating is nothing if not a series of tests and quizzes, graded informally and weighted according to an individual set of criteria. Your job, when trying to figure out who might be a good long-term candidate, is to know—to the best of your ability—the criteria you're basing your judgments upon. Most of the time, we rely too heavily on pure instinct. Although that can be a stunningly accurate tool, it's very easy to doubt oneself afterward. We can make the mistake of talking ourselves out of following our heart (or our gut) if we don't look deeply enough into WHY we want what we want from a life partner. So, before you begin scoring the behavior of your potential mates, you first need to create your*

individual test key..."

This was the tough part, but the author made her point very well. It *was* easy to second guess a decision based on pure logic. My mind was telling me that Grant was a better choice and, on paper, he was.

But my instincts were saying something else. My heart and my gut were both telling me that I felt most like *myself* when I was with...well, almost anyone else.

I didn't know Chance Michaelsen well enough outside of the gym, but when I thought of him, I smiled. Not only because he was handsome and talented at his job and kind, but because he was really looking at me when we talked. I couldn't hide myself from him with a veil of polite smiles and facile words. He would notice.

I wasn't sure I could say the same about Grant, but I fully intended to look specifically for that trait on our date tomorrow. It would be my biggest relationship test for the two of us so far.

❀❀❀

The waters of Lake Michigan sparkled with glints of chipped sapphire on this crisp, cold, and clear Friday afternoon in mid-April. Grant Jordan was standing next to me on the outer deck of the luxury yacht he'd hired to take us on this daytime cruise.

It was spectacular, if more than a little brisk when we stepped outside of the toasty cabin. But I'd requested fresh air, so here we were.

"Like it?" Grant asked.

"Who wouldn't?" I replied. "We have a gorgeous spring day, a free afternoon together, and a stunning view of the lake, the shore, and the city skyline. I'm very impressed, Grant."

A smile lit his handsome face. "Glad you approve."

He reached for my hand and held it on the deck as we huddled next to one another and leaned on the metal railing. He talked about some of the things he enjoyed about the city of Chicago—from the Midwestern openness to the cultural diversity—and even some of the things he liked about me. He was attracted to me. Thought I was intelligent, warm, hardworking, and independent. Who would be immune to such compliments?

So, it was lovely for a while. Really lovely. And I was talking myself into it again—being with Grant. I'd been excited to see him during the daytime, mostly because that meant he'd taken off work for me. To be with *me*.

But it was a strange thing...attention. It waxed and waned and, with Grant, it waned much more than waxed.

Especially when his cell phone would buzz.

Even if I didn't see or hear it, I could feel him responding to it. He might be technically spending time with me, but he was no more attentive really than he'd been before, at the Thai restaurant or during our prior dates. He liked me, but he didn't crave me. He didn't make me a top priority over other things in his life, not even for a few hours. I could feel him ready to spring back into action for work, just as soon as he could. He was always ready to jump into the business world again. It made me wonder, did he appreciate my independence so much because he figured it would be a necessary trait for anyone in a long-term relationship with him?

"I've got the rest of the day planned," he told me, "so I hope you'll be able to stay a while tonight. André is throwing together something good for us to eat."

"I wouldn't miss it," I said, feeling momentarily hopeful. Maybe he just needed more time to decompress than most people. Maybe it just took him longer to truly relax.

See? It was back and forth and back and forth—these

arguments in my mind. Grant was trying. That had to count for something, right?

After we disembarked, he took me to his place for dinner...and by "place" I meant "mansion." I'd been here before a couple of times already, but the magnitude of it struck me anew each time. The well-kept grounds. The gazillion rooms. The pricey furnishings. Part of me wished those things meant more to me than they did. The house was notable, striking, and imposing. But it wasn't anywhere I'd want to be alone for days at a time. Or years. And, if my relationship with Grant were to progress as far as I'd once wished it would, I would be alone. A lot.

Grant had a live-in French cook (naturally). And the dinner André "threw together" for us was rather extraordinary. There was tender veal with some kind of special sauce. Asparagus spears cooked to perfection. A mixed salad of baby greens with sliced peaches and strawberries, tossed in a citrus dressing. Red potatoes sliced and pan fried with spices. And a melt-in-your-mouth cherry cobbler for dessert with a scoop of French vanilla custard on top.

It was all delicious, but it was the after-dinner "menu" that I was most curious about. I couldn't eat another bite, but I was hoping Grant would find something else for us to do with our mouths... Was he going to finally make a romantic move?

"Do you have a favorite type of music, Nia? Something you'd like to listen to tonight?"

"I love all different styles," I told him. "What about you? What do you most enjoy?"

He shrugged. "I usually just put on a classical station. Not because I'm a Bach or Mozart aficionado, but because I like not having the words there. Lyrics tend to break my concentration."

"Interesting," I said, but I immediately thought of Chance at the gym on Wednesday afternoon. There were a lot of songs with lyrics that touched my emotions in some way. And that last one we heard together, "Let Love In," was meaningful. I thought Chance and I had a little moment, actually, when that song came on the radio. He wasn't a man who was particularly gushy. He usually played his emotions very close to the vest. But the expression in his eyes when I defended him against Donna's bitchy comments was like an hour of conversation condensed into just one look.

"Would you like to dance?" Grant asked me.

I grinned. "Sure." He'd put on some sort of Viennese waltz that made me feel like I was on the set of a BBC period drama. I mean, I was more Black Eyed Peas than Brahms, but I could play along with this scene, if that was what Grant liked.

He held out his hand, and I took it. He drew me toward him and, soon, our bodies were flush. But Grant was so poised. So very...competent. I supposed that wasn't a traditionally *sexy* thought to have about my boyfriend, but it was true. Grant was the kind of man that looked like he could pull off a complicated business merger, run a board meeting blindfolded, and select the perfect appetizer for a party—simultaneously—without breaking a sweat.

Somewhere in the middle of the musical movement, he stopped dancing and let his hands slide upward to cradle my face. He ran the pad of his thumb lightly over my lips, smiled, and brought his mouth down on mine.

Like everything else about Grant Jordan, his kiss was polished and well practiced. He'd kissed me in passing a dozen times and, on a few occasions, went a little deeper. But I was far too aware that I should be wanting more right now. I should not be objectively analyzing his kiss as if I were grading an assignment or rating a project according to a 100-point rubric.

I thought of the pink book and all of the relationship tests and quizzes, and I barely suppressed a shudder. What was wrong with me that I couldn't feel more for this brilliant, attractive, and successful man?

Then, I felt a surprising vibration against my hip and, for a split second, I thought, *Whoa, there!* And hoped that, perhaps, I'd been too hasty in dismissing the potential for a strong sexual chemistry with Grant.

But he pulled away from me, and my brain and my body both finally understood that this brief zip of excitement was just his cell phone buzzing. Again. My hope for us dissolved the instant he said, "Apologies, Nia. I need to grab this call quick." And my determination to change the course of the evening intensified.

While Grant spoke with some business person on the phone, I excused myself and slipped into the bathroom—a palatial one, especially for a man who technically lived alone. (Although, I guess he had enough live-in staff to justify it, eh?) I didn't need a lot of space, however, for what I intended to do. Just privacy.

I pulled out my own cell phone and texted Chance Michaelsen before I could talk myself out of it. I wrote:

If you get this message, could you please call my cell in about 10 minutes? Just go with whatever I say.

Fifteen seconds later, my phone dinged, and Chance texted back:

You got it.

Oh, boy. I'd set this in motion...was it too late to go back on it?

Well, I guess it wasn't. I could ignore the call when it came in or change what I'd planned to say...but, as it turned out, I didn't want to.

Would I live to regret my decision, though? Maybe. Only time would tell.

Grant was waiting for me when I stepped out of the bathroom. "European distributors," he explained with a wave of his hand. "There shouldn't be any other interruptions for a while."

I appreciated his optimistic comment, but I knew it wasn't entirely true. No matter how much Grant wished he could relax and spend time with me, he just wasn't built that way. I couldn't help but feel that it wasn't even his fault. He was like a shark who had to keep swimming (and working, and checking his iPhone) or he'd die. Being still simply wasn't an option for him, and the people he worked with knew it. That was why they kept calling. They knew he'd respond.

The sad truth was that, even if he eventually came to love me with his whole heart, and vice versa, this wouldn't change. No amount of love could alter such a fundamental trait in another person.

"Life partners can and should learn to compromise on the details of daily living, but neither partner should ever be expected to change his/her own identity or to try to force the other to change his/her core self," the author of the pink book had written.

I was starting to resent and despise the author of the pink book, but I couldn't deny that her research and wisdom were frequently accurate.

Grant leaned in to kiss me again, and I tried one last time to relax into his embrace. To feel more than I did. But it was no use.

When my cell phone rang, I literally leapt to answer it.

"It's my brother," I told Grant. Which was, of course, a massive lie. "Hi, Dimitri," I said, answering the call.

"Hey, there...uh, *Sis,*" Chance said.

I smiled and then paused, pretending to listen to my "brother's" side of the conversation. Grant was preoccupied halfway across the room, scrolling through some texts or emails on his own phone.

I swallowed, forced myself to look more serious, and said into my cell, "Really? How short staffed are we?" I paused again.

Chance said, *"Very."*

"But Mama's doing okay?" I waited for a reply.

"I'm going to guess that she's rapidly improving," Chance finally said. "She needed her rest."

"No, Dimitri," I replied. "I'm not at all surprised that she's resting now. Those migraines really wipe her out. Can you handle The Gala alone or do you need me to come back."

"I need you to come back. Now," Chance said, his voice more amused than I would have liked.

I glanced at Grant, who looked over at me with concern. But then he turned his attention back to his cell phone.

Until now, I'd been debating whether or not I'd follow through and actually leave. Grant's nonverbal indifference pushed me to make my decision.

"Okay. I'll come home right away. See you soon, Dimitri."

"Very soon, I hope," Chance replied with a low chuckle.

I clicked off my phone. "I'm so sorry, Grant. My family needs my help at The Gala tonight. I'm glad I got to spend such a wonderful afternoon and evening with you, though. The lake cruise and dinner here—it was wonderful," I said, and I meant it sincerely.

"I understand," he said. "I'll drive you back to the dock so you can get your car."

"Thank you."

I let out a sigh of relief when I was safely back in my own vehicle. Grant was a decent and honorable man, but I could tell he wasn't too disappointed about my leaving. He had people to connect with and messages to respond to. And, as it turned out, so did I.

There was a text waiting for me on my phone. I pulled into an abandoned store parking lot a few miles away to answer it. Chance had written:

Heading back to Mirabelle Harbor?

I texted back:
Yes. Thanks for helping me.
He replied:
Anytime.
Then, ten seconds later, he added:
Meet me at the gym.

Was he serious about making up the workout session I'd missed today? I couldn't really go home yet. It wasn't even eight-thirty, and my family didn't expect me to return until eleven-thirty or midnight tonight. If I got back this early, there'd be too many questions. I'd be dealing with enough of an inquisition when I told them later that I wasn't going to continue to date Grant.

To Chance, I wrote:
I don't feel like working out. Besides, I'm not dressed for it.

As if he'd anticipated my reaction, his reply came back within seconds:
There's more than one kind of workout, Nia. Clothing can be optional.

My mouth dropped open. Well, I couldn't just leave it at that, could I? So, I texted:
Are you propositioning me?

His reply was swift:
Not yet. If I were propositioning you, I'd say to meet me at my apartment. But I said to meet me at the gym.

This was followed by a smiley emoticon and the words:
I'll be waiting.

Curiosity about what he was up to and what he might have in mind for tonight left me a little breathless. I responded:
Fine. I'm on my way.
Then I started driving again.

When I got to Harbor Fitness, there was a guy sitting at the front desk that I'd never seen before—probably because I'd never been in here at night. Aside from him, there were only a few hardcore exercisers on the treadmills and weight machines.

And then I saw Chance, leaning up against the doorframe to the employees' lounge behind the desk. When I walked up to the front, he smiled.

"Glad you could make it, Nia," he said. Then, to the other guy, he added, "I'm grabbing a couple of towels, Raj. And this." He dangled a key from his fingers.

Raj nodded. "No prob. See ya later, man." He and Chance fist bumped.

There was a wire rack with laundered and folded white towels behind Raj. Chance snatched two large, fluffy ones and pointed toward the locker rooms.

I'd always come already dressed for my workout sessions, so I hadn't needed to go into the women's locker room before. Chance handed me a towel and said, "Take off as much as you want and wrap yourself up in this. Then meet me in here."

He indicated a wooden door that was situated exactly between both locker rooms and labeled "SAUNA." With the key he was holding, Chance unlocked the door, raised an eyebrow at me with a look of challenge, and said, "See you inside." Then he strolled into the men's locker room with his own towel.

Oh, my...

I mentally skimmed the text he'd written a half hour ago. *There's more than one kind of workout, Nia. Clothing can be optional.* I laughed. Chance Michaelsen was a deceptively clever man. And a sensual one. He understood the art of foreplay.

I undressed quickly, leaving on just my panties, and wrapped myself up in the large towel. Everything else, I secured in one of the metal lockers.

Chance was already sitting in the warm sauna, his towel wrapped securely around his waist, when I slipped into the room.

"It's going to take a few minutes to heat up in here," he told me. "We keep the thermostat off unless a client requests some steam."

Chance was mistaken. It was already *very* hot in the sauna, and it was getting hotter by the second. After all, I was standing just a few feet away from the guy and he wasn't wearing a shirt. I could see every single ripple of well-defined muscle in his chest. I considered it an act of extreme self restraint that I didn't reach out and run my palm across his pecs and abs and whatever else caught my eye.

"I suppose this is easier than doing weight exercises," I said. *But only technically.* I sat gingerly on one of the benches across from him and tried to keep from staring at him. Whenever I looked too closely at his torso, I felt like I was running a fever.

He laughed. "Maybe. But an occasional sauna cleanse is a good thing for your body, too. Opens up the pores. Relaxes the muscles. Removes the toxins. And, best of all, it can give the mind a break."

I nodded. As I settled back further on the bench, feeling the temperature in the room really spiking now, I was just beginning to realize how long it had been since I'd been able to sit still, let go of my body's tension, and just *be*.

I pulled my hair back off my neck and away from the beads of sweat that were forming there. Chance's eyes watched me as I fashioned a little twist and tucked the hair carefully so it would stay up.

"Cool how you can do that," he said, "without a mirror or a hair clip or anything."

"It's not a big deal," I said with a shrug. But I couldn't dismiss Chance's gaze. He was watching my every movement, noticing each inch of exposed skin, which wasn't much on my side, really. The white towels gave comprehensive coverage. They were jumbo sized, so only my shoulders, arms, lower thighs, calves, and feet were visible.

But Chance took in every bit, and I squirmed under that level of scrutiny.

We sat in silence for a long time.

Finally, he cleared his throat. "So, Nia, is Grant Jordan still your boyfriend?"

I shook my head. I hadn't said any official breakup words to Grant, which would really be more like, "Hey, I don't think we should hang out for a few hours during the weekend anymore." Our relationship had hardly been the stuff of soulmates. But, after tonight, I knew I didn't want to go back to Grant's large but lonely mansion.

"My parents liked him a lot, though," I explained to Chance. "They'll be disappointed."

He narrowed his eyes. "Are *you* disappointed?"

"No."

He abruptly stood up and walked over to me. With no shirt fabric as a shield, there was nothing that could camouflage his incredibly buff upper body. Bet he did more than torso twists to get that six pack, huh? Even more than wanting to touch him, though, I wanted to know what he was thinking. My attention kept getting drawn back to his face. To his inquisitive hazel eyes.

He stood in front of me and pulled me to standing. "Turn around," he whispered.

"Why?" I murmured, glancing at the door. There was an oval sliver of a window where people walking by could peek in on us, if they were so inclined.

"I'm going to rub your shoulders," he said simply. "Don't worry. I'll stop anytime you want, but now's the best time to loosen those tight muscles. You can lean against the wall for balance."

There was almost nothing in the world I wanted more than to feel Chance's hands on my skin. Between his nearness to me, my anticipation of his touch, and the blazing temperature of the sauna, I could only take quick, shallow breaths but, nevertheless, I turned around.

From the very second his fingertips connected with the top of my shoulders, it was all I could do not to gasp or moan. He had magic hands, that man. A grip that was strong, firm, but not pinching. My neck and shoulders had never felt better.

I could only imagine what he could do to my back if I were to throw the towel on the floor and let him rub whatever he wanted, or wherever he wanted. Aunt Helen would be evoking all kinds of prayers to the blessed Virgin if she knew what I was thinking.

"You really missed your calling," I managed to say.

Chance made that low chuckling sound that sent a bolt of desire from my ears to my toenails. "I have some background in deep tissue and Swedish massage," he told me. "Board certified, actually. But I'm very selective in choosing my clientele for that service."

The air in the sauna must have hit about three thousand degrees when he spoke. I was burning up. But he continued to rub only above the towel line. Nothing remotely inappropriate. And his self-control made me want to scream, "Go lower! Push the towel down, Chance. Tell me you want me half as much as I want you."

Instead, I just sighed, and his fingers stilled. *No!*

He very gently turned me around to face him, lowered his head until his lips were millimeters from mine, and whispered, "Number 127 Arpeggio Avenue. Apartment 3."

"What?" I asked. There was steam all around us and, more than that, my brain was in a fog.

"That's my address. Just two blocks south of here." He paused. "It's your choice, Nia. But remember your question when we were texting tonight? When you asked if I was propositioning you?"

I nodded.

Oh, yes. I remembered.

If I were propositioning you, I'd say to meet me at my apartment...

"So," he said slowly, "if you would like, meet me at my apartment." Then Chance smiled, stepped away from me, and walked out of the sauna.

CHAPTER EIGHT

~*Chance*~

Jogging with a hard-on was painful, I discovered, but only part of my problem was physical.

As I raced back to my apartment, lit a few candles, and tuned my stereo on low to LOVE FM, the only thought in my mind was, "Would Nia show up?"

I didn't trust my clock. I stared at it until it flipped to the next number. How could one minute take so damned long? Was it running slow? The minutes ticked by with the speed of a comatose glacier. Seventeen minutes. Nineteen minutes. Twenty-three freakin' minutes.

Then there was a soft knock on my door.

Thank you. Glad to know there really *was* a God.

I opened the door.

"May I come in?" Nia asked sweetly. She was so proper, so polite. But I looked closely at her expression. There was a fire in her dark eyes that had me wanting to yank her into my apartment and take her immediately to bed.

But I only said, "Absolutely," and ushered her into my

living room.

She glanced around, taking it all in. "You're a minimalist." She smiled, but she spoke the truth. I wasn't much into accumulating stuff.

"I like to keep it simple."

"Apparently," she said. "I like it, though. It's streamlined and classic. It's a style that fits you."

She began to meander around my place. There wasn't much to it—I lived in a one-bedroom, after all—so her self-directed tour didn't last long. I just stood off to the side, near my black leather sofa, which was my only major piece of furniture in the room, and I watched her. Better than any weekend movie.

But she soon returned to me. I waited for her to speak. I didn't trust myself.

"Nice candles," she observed. I'd lit just a handful of vanilla-scented ones, small but luminous. "And I like the music, too."

Yeah. *"Nothing but love, 24/7,"* or so the slogan went.

"Thanks." I pointed toward the kitchen counter, where I'd set out two long-stemmed glasses and a bottle of shiraz. "Wine?"

She shook her head and stepped right up to me then, our bodies only a few inches apart. Generally, I wasn't fond of people of either gender or from any culture invading my personal space. This feeling, however, did not apply to Nia Pappayiannis.

Move in closer, sweetheart.

"No wine," she whispered. "Just you." She looked up at me with a sense of anticipation. Expectation. Longing.

Okay, then. I'd been hoping for a clear signal, and here it was. Green light.

So, I reached out to touch her hair. It was still up in that mysterious twist thing she did with it in the sauna. I tugged at it until those beautiful dark strands tumbled down around her face. And then finally, finally I moved in to kiss her.

It was like I'd been waiting for a decade for our lips to touch. She arched up against me as I gathered her closer. God, it wasn't nearly close enough, though. I drank her in, pulling at her mouth with mine and taking in her very breath. When she moaned, I wasn't sure I'd ever been so proud of an accomplishment in my life.

After our time in the sauna, she'd put back on her fancy outfit from her date with that superficial CEO. Nothing wrong with the dress but, man, did I ever want her out of it.

"I'm itching to tear this fabric off of you," I confessed. "So, if you think you'll ever want to wear this outfit again, you might want to remove it. Quickly."

She laughed, unfastened some latch or something behind her back, and stepped out of the dress.

It took my breath away to see her in only her bra and panties. She had such smooth and beautiful olive skin—I stared at her, temporarily dazed.

She yanked at my shirt. I didn't resist as she pulled it off of me. "Get rid of these," she said, pointing at my jeans. "And meet me in your bedroom."

She sauntered away from me with the most angelic smile I'd ever seen on a woman's face. Then she paused and added, "I plan to have my wicked way with you."

I snapped out of my trance, ditched my jeans in the middle of the living room floor, and followed her.

~*Nia*~

To the sound of Edwin McCain's "I'll Be" on the radio, Chance Michaelsen and I finally made love. And, oh, dear Lord, it was worth the wait.

He trailed kisses down both sides of my neck, then devoured my mouth again. He raked his hands down my back with such expert pressure that any pain I may once have felt was gone like a whisper.

He was all limbs and lean muscle. I couldn't stop

touching him. Marveling at the beauty of his body.

And at long last I got to run my palms across those amazing abs of his and feel the waves of muscular strength beneath his skin.

"You like that area, huh?" he asked, breathless between kisses.

"Oh, yeah," I said. We were on our sides, face to face, legs entwined, but I kept leaning back a bit...the better to see and touch him.

He made a sound that was half laugh, half groan. "Then you should be on top this time, shouldn't you?"

Before I had a chance to move or even think, he grabbed me and lifted me onto him in one swift movement so I was straddling his hips.

"Now you can touch my chest as much as you want," he said. "And I can touch yours."

"Oh," I moaned, as he positioned me just where he wanted and then pulled me down—fully—onto him. He stroked me upward from my legs to my waist to my breasts. And I stroked him downward from his neck to his shoulders to his chest. And then we clung to each other, riding and rocking yet again.

He had so much physicality combined with skill and control that I was aware I was in the presence of a true athlete. And when he folded himself around me, brought me down side by side with him again, and cradled me in his arms, I felt utterly protected. Completely safe and secure.

We rested for a while and, maybe, napped—I'd completely lost track of time. Chance hadn't stopped holding me, though, or rubbing my arms, my hips, my chest.

He whispered, "You have beautiful breasts, Nia."

"Thanks, but—"

"But what?"

Okay, this was embarrassing. I'd been too passion crazed in the moments before to have cared, but self-consciousness was returning. His body was so trim, so hard. Mine was...a lot less so.

"But what, Nia? You can tell me."

"But don't you think they're too big? That my body is too squishy?"

"No." He chuckled. "Not at all. I think you're gorgeous. Perfect."

I smiled. "No one's perfect, Chance."

"You're right. If you were perfect, you'd shut up and let me kiss you again."

And so we alternated kissing and fondling. Stroking, riding, and holding each other for as long as we could. Until we were both exhausted but satiated. Until sleep finally became too irresistible to deny.

❁❀❁

I was startled awake by an unfamiliar brightness. "What's that light?" I asked, squinting.

"Probably my window," Chance murmured.

"Your window..." I repeated, slowly opening my eyes up to a room I had no recollection of ever seeing. It had been dark when I'd come in here a few hours ago. I'd seen only shadows and hadn't bothered to guess at the room's contents beyond the bed. And Chance following me into it.

Now, in the growing light, I saw a dresser, too, the door to a closet, an assortment of garments—mine and his—scattered on the floor, along with a handful of hastily ripped open condom wrappers. But, otherwise, it was as sparsely decorated as the rest of his apartment. One framed family photograph on the dresser. One small nightstand with a lamp and a clock.

A clock.

I read the time. "Oh, my God, Chance, it's 6:18!"

"Yeah?"

I bolted upright, narrowly missing the bottom of his chin with my head. "I'm going to be in so much trouble. I've got to go home *now*."

He pushed himself up onto his elbow and stared at me. "Seriously? You're twenty-six. You have a curfew?"

Ack. How to explain this to a guy who wasn't from an Old World family?

"Not exactly. But it's disrespectful not to let your parents know that you're going to be out all night when you're still living in their house."

He tilted his head but continued staring. "Understood. But I sense there's more to this."

I nodded. "It was too early for me to go home after I ended my date with Grant last night—there would have been too many questions—but I didn't expect to stay out so late with you either." I got out of bed and began the search for my clothing around his apartment. It was like a scavenger hunt, trying to find all the pieces.

"And?"

"And, so, my parents are early risers. I'll not only have to answer to being out all night with a man, but they're going to assume that Grant was the man I was with."

"We don't want that," Chance said, smiling.

"No, we don't." But Chance didn't know the half of it. My parents *liked* Grant. A lot. I'd done a fabulous job of selling that relationship to them, dammit. I doubted they even knew who Chance Michaelsen was, apart from his recognizable last name. He'd never set foot in The Gala. He didn't eat Greek food. He wasn't one for backslapping, hugging, or other excessive shows of emotion. Even getting him to smile took some effort. They'd have no flipping idea what to do with a creature like him.

I grabbed my phone and checked for messages. One missed text from Dimitri (the *real* one), sent this morning at 5:32. My brother wrote:

Are you dead or just getting laid? Mama's been pacing

for half an hour in the living room.

Oh, no.

I texted back:

I'm alive...just fell asleep. Heading home now.

Finally, I managed to collect my clothing and put it on. My hair was beyond fixing, although I gave finger-combing it into another twist my best shot. But I'd had really great sex last night, and it showed.

"I have to go," I told Chance.

He'd gotten out of bed, too, and thrown on his boxers. I wanted to rip them off and chase him back onto the mattress.

"I know," he said, sighing. And then he kissed me until I was sure I wouldn't want to leave until noon. The next day. Or maybe the next week.

"Bye," I whispered, forcing myself to step away.

"See you soon," he said.

I hoped that was a promise. However, it was one that should probably wait until after I'd managed to break the news to my parents that their fantasies of my future engagement to a certain popular CEO wouldn't actually be happening.

And the thought of Aunt Helen—along with all of her prayers for me and my many future children—had me cringing as I drove home.

CHAPTER NINE

~*Nia*~

I knew it was futile to try to slip into the house unseen or unheard. Mama had the vision and hearing of a woman three decades younger—and the imagination of a fantasy writer. There were going to be questions, so I'd better be ready for them.

"You usually call if you'll be out all night, Antonia," Mama said from her semi-hidden perch on the staircase nearest the doorway.

I nodded. "I'm so sorry I worried you. I was really tired last night and just fell asleep."

"I know," she said. "Dimitri told me you'd texted him." Then she smiled. "So, it's serious between you two, then, yes? You're in love with Grant." She clapped her hands together, not waiting for me to reply. "I'm so excited for you, sweetheart. He will make you a wonderful husband! But, perhaps, we'd better not tell your father that you were out with him all night until after your engagement, eh?" She pointed upstairs and I could hear the shower running. "He just got up and didn't know you'd stayed out so late.

Quick, quick. Go change into, um—" She scanned my disheveled outfit. "Something else. And, maybe, brush your hair."

But though she spoke urgently and practically pushed me out of the room before I could even attempt an explanation, there was a twinkling in her eyes that was unmistakable. And I realized I was in much bigger trouble than I'd thought.

Way over my head, in fact.

It was going to be a major problem getting them to like Chance after this. Not when my very traditional mother (who generally disapproved of premarital sex) wasn't even upset about me sleeping with a man out of wedlock— provided that man was Grant Jordan.

I dutifully changed, washed up, brushed my hair and my teeth, and tried to figure out how to turn the Titanic around so it wouldn't hit that iceberg.

Here was the thing—I loved my mother and all my family. I knew they wanted only what was best for me. However, they were worried about me. Worried I'd be "an old maid" if they didn't succeed in getting me married off before I turned thirty.

Between my mom, my aunts, my cousins, and various friends of the family, I'd already been introduced to every "nice Greek boy" in the Midwest and, much to my parents' disappointment, hadn't wanted to marry any of them.

No one in the world would consider a man like Grant Jordan to be a consolation prize, though. So, on some level, I knew the second I'd started dating him that, if I wasn't going to marry someone who was actually Greek, at least he was a guy my family would understand my relationship with. In truth, it had been part of my attraction to him. And I was horrified to realize that, for the sake of family harmony, I probably would have been able to subvert my own lack of sexual desire for Grant if I hadn't met Chance Michaelsen.

What kind of a person was I that I'd be willing to ignore my own instincts?

And how could I possibly explain to my parents what had changed in me if I didn't fully understand it myself?

When I got back downstairs, I kissed my father good morning. Mama was fixing coffee for us all. My brother was still in his bedroom. From the outside, it looked like a normal Saturday morning in the Pappayiannis house.

"We have a busy day ahead," my dad declared. "Somebody better wake up Dimitri. It's time to get to work."

❀✸❀

I tried to lose myself in baking tasks—rolling up the *dolmades*, crimping the edges of the feta *piroskis*, sautéing the meat for the *moussaka*—but Chance was on my mind all day. I couldn't get him out of my head.

He'd invaded my senses so much that I could still see, hear, taste, and smell him. And feel him, too. The way he'd touched me. The way I'd touched him.

When he first followed me into his bedroom last night, all he said was, "I did as you asked."

Sure enough, he'd ditched the jeans. There was, however, still the matter of his boxers.

He was leaning against the doorframe, looking at me as I lounged on his bed in only my underwear. The light was behind him, so his face was in shadow and I couldn't read his expression. I was aware, though, that he wasn't laughing at me or judging me. That he was simply waiting for me to direct him in whatever I'd wanted to have happen next.

I'd already told him—oh, so boldly—that I planned to have my wicked way with him. For a man with such physical power, the fact that he completely let me take the lead gave me an unexpected bolt of confidence.

"Are you going to join me, or do I have to drag you over here?" I asked.

I could feel, rather than see, his grin.

He walked to the bed with the graceful prowl of a wildcat and climbed onto the mattress with me. Then he trailed his fingertips slowly from my thigh up to my shoulder, leaving only a delicious tingle in the wake of his touch. I knew he could possess me in the span of a heartbeat. And yet, he still held back. Inviting me to make my move.

I reached for his boxers and tugged at the waistband. "I want to take these off of you," I said, easing them down slowly to the tops of his muscular thighs. Then I added, "Now, lie down and hold still."

Admiring the exposed skin, the impressive erection, the control that kept him on his back, trusting me with whatever I planned to do, I slid the thin boxers off all the way and began exploring him with my mouth. With a series of licks and kisses that had him gripping the bed sheet and breathing unevenly, I'd miraculously managed to pin him down without a single arm or leg restraint. Just my instructions.

This power and freedom he'd given me came with a deep desire to justify his trust. I wanted to be worthy of it. To pleasure him intensely.

"Slower?" I asked. "Or faster?"

"Nia," he ground out. "I'm already yours. You can set the pace."

I remembered laughing at that and hearing his hoarse chuckle in return.

"I just want you so much," I admitted, kissing more of his body, all of the skin I'd never seen until tonight. He squirmed a little. He moaned a lot. But, mostly, he just let me torment him with my lips until I couldn't take not having him touch me, too.

"Do you have a condom I can put on you?" I asked.

"Oh, God. Yes."

He reached behind him, opened a drawer on his nightstand, and handed me a foil packet. I made quick work of rolling the rubber on him. Then I paused, wondering how best to articulate what I most desired. "All I want is for you to touch me," I whispered. "And to be fully with me."

"You're going to let me move now, right?" he asked.

"Right."

The wildcat sprang into action. Somehow in the space of under five seconds he'd unlatched my bra, flipped me to my back, and begun suckling on my breasts. I felt the tugging deep inside my body and arched up to be closer to his mouth. For ages I'd longed to be with a man who was really *attentive* to me. No doubt about it—I'd found him.

I couldn't even remember when he'd gotten rid of my panties, just that it happened fairly soon. But I was so wet from wanting him that when his fingers stroked me, I cried out, "Oh, c'mon, Chance!"

"Say what you need," he whispered in my ear.

"I need you to be inside me."

I felt his smile against my cheek as he thrust into me the first time. And then the second. And then the third. I came within moments. And almost immediately I wanted him again.

I'd been waiting an eternity to be made love to like that. I couldn't imagine living without this kind of passion and—

"Nia, wake up," Dimitri said, snapping his fingers a few inches from my nose.

"What?" I said to my brother. He was trying to pull away from the table the finished pan of *moussaka* that I'd been working on. I'd apparently been gripping the edges of the metal pan too tightly.

"We need to bake this," he said in that "my sister is as

dumb as a rock" tone, which I knew so well from years of siblinghood.

"Fine. Take it." I released my hold on the pan and turned my fingers over to some other cooking task. Anything to keep myself busy.

"Your head is somewhere else today, Nia. What are you daydreaming about?" Dimitri paused. "You know what? Never mind. I don't wanna know."

He and I were alone in the kitchen, while Mama and Papa were out front dealing with the customers. The restaurant wouldn't be serving until lunch time, but the bakery was always open early.

I appreciated not having the scrutiny of my parents on me this morning, but it wasn't as though my brother was making my life easy or anything.

I got up and began to walk around the table, breathing deeply and stretching my back, just the way Chance had shown me at the gym. All that muscle strengthening and preventative care was beginning to work. I'd noticed that, around Chance, I'd become more aware of my body. More knowledgeable of its needs—and not just in a sexual sense. I was remembering to take more breaks, keep a better posture, notice an uncomfortable motion before it created a painful ache. And I'd only completed half of the workout sessions so far. What would I learn in the second half?

Out in the bakery, I could hear the chattering of voices and loud greetings for the regulars. It was the usual weekend chaos. Scores of people came in on Saturday morning to pick up treats for afternoon or evening events.

"We're running low on baklava," my mother informed me, popping into the kitchen for a few minutes to grab some extra *souvlaki* skewers.

So, next up: Make more baklava.

The food prep kept me occupied during the lunch hours and beyond. I no longer had to waitress—my parents had an easier time hiring out for that than for the other tasks.

They needed me to help primarily with the cooking. Although The Gala had a relatively small menu, consisting almost entirely of Greek specialties, every item had to be made just right. The Grecian way. It was authenticity that kept customers coming back.

I'd just finished taking another quick stretching break that late afternoon, once the worst of the Saturday rush had calmed, when my father poked his head into the kitchen.

"Your boyfriend is here," he said. Then Papa disappeared back into the bakery.

In my addled mind, exhausted from hours of work and running only on caffeine and less than four hours of sleep last night, the only thought that propelled me from my kitchen workstation out into the public was, "How did my dad already know Chance was my boyfriend?"

Because, honestly, it didn't even occur to me—until I saw Grant Jordan standing there—that I might see him today. That Grant would just show up unannounced at my family's restaurant. Not even once had we gotten together without an advanced plan. Never two days in a row.

But there he was. Looking dashing in his designer "casual" clothes. And holding a bouquet of flowers.

I stared at him. "Grant?"

"Hi, Nia," he said brightly. Then he handed the flowers to my mother. "These are for you," he said to her. "I'm glad to see you're feeling better today."

Oh, busted!

Mama shot me a puzzled look, but I must have looked panicky enough that she decided to take pity on me and play along. "Why, um...thank you, Grant. Let me just put this beautiful bouquet in some water." And she turned her back on him before sending me another confused look.

I cleared my throat. "It's such a...uh, big surprise to see you here, Grant. How are you doing today?"

He walked over to where I was standing, kissed me lightly on the cheek, and said, "Better now. You had to leave so early last night. I missed you."

To this, my brother raised one dark bushy eyebrow. Thankfully, he said nothing.

"Likewise," I murmured.

Then, turning to my father, Grant said, "I don't know if you can spare Nia for the evening, but I have two tickets to a Parkside Pavilion concert tonight. It's a classical ensemble, led by New York conductor Jeremiah Wilhelm, featuring Russian pianist Alexi Broturakov and a Chinese string quartet led by violinist Li Li Ming." He grinned and waved the tickets at me.

"Wow," I said. I'd never heard of any of these musicians. And I was so tired, I'd probably snooze through their performances.

"They're box seats," Grant continued, "but I thought we could have dinner at a cute Italian place nearby and drink some wine before the concert starts."

"That sounds lovely, Grant, but—" I waved at my family members. "It's still really busy here, so..."

"She would love to," Papa said for me, nodding at Grant.

My mouth dropped open.

"She has been working very hard today," Mama agreed. "This sounds like a very nice thing, wouldn't you say so, Antonia?"

"Well, yes," I said, "but I—"

"All settled then!" my father exclaimed. "Now, Grant, before you two go, let me show you something. When you were here last week, we were talking about the ouzo made in Athens, yes?"

"Yes, of course," Grant said. "That distillery you really liked, right?"

"We got in a fresh shipment on Wednesday," Papa said. "You come and try some. Just a tiny bit. Back here." He motioned for Grant to go into the storage room with him.

The Chicago CEO said, "Opa!" much to my parents'

delight and, with a quick wink in my direction, followed my dad into the backroom.

Dimitri crossed his arms and gazed at me. "What's the story, Nia?" he whispered.

I just shook my head and rubbed my temples with my fingertips.

Mama was making some weird *tsking* sound and staring at me strangely. "The thing I don't understand—" she began.

The door jingled as a new customer came in.

"Hello, Nia," the male voice I'd been hearing in my head all day long said to me.

"Chance," I whispered. "H-Hi, there."

"I was just...walking by," he said. "And thought I'd see how you were doing." He smiled at me and gave Dimitri and Mama a very polite nod each.

It was immediate, I realized. The pull of the attraction I'd felt for him was so strong, even in this awkward situation. I hadn't been hallucinating it. It wasn't even twelve hours later, and I still wanted him so much. A look of recognition—and pure white heat—passed between us.

"Oh, uh," I finally said. "Chance, this is my brother Dimitri and my mother Sophia. Everyone, I'd like you to meet Chance Michaelsen. He's Sharlene's brother and also my personal trainer. At the gym."

Dimitri and my mom both said a warm hello, but I knew them. They were watching Chance like a pair of hawks. Taking in his mannerisms and all of his nonverbal signals.

He looked weirdly out of place and uncomfortable in our family bakery. Like someone unfamiliar with drugs might look when faced with shelves filled with pharmaceuticals.

My brother narrowed his eyes and glanced between us.

Mama squinted at our new customer for a long, long moment and then sent me a look that assured me she was no fool. That the puzzle pieces that had perplexed her before had finally fallen into place.

She said to Chance, "We have samples of baklava right here. My daughter just made it. Come! You try a piece."

Chance swallowed and took a step back from the bakery counter. "Oh, no, I couldn't. I'm sure it's delicious, but I—I just ate."

Oh, my God. His first meeting with my Greek mother and he refused a food offering. This did not bode well.

"Just a *little* piece then?" she asked.

"Again, thank you," he said. "But I'm really full."

Mama didn't understand this mystifying concept of 'not having room for dessert.' She stared at Chance as if he were a lime-green, two-headed alien from somewhere just to the left of the Andromeda Galaxy.

And he, poor guy, didn't realize how unintentionally insulting he'd just been. How this would not be an easy bridge to repair now. I hadn't had the opportunity to warn him or coach him, like I would have if I'd been ready for him to visit us here. Ready to introduce him to my family as my boyfriend.

It was, of course, in that moment that Grant and Papa emerged from the backroom, laughing like schoolboys and smelling of licorice-flavored alcohol.

"So, Nia, you and your boyfriend must go have fun now!" my father said, slapping Grant on the back and laughing some more. "He will take good care of you tonight."

Grant, who was carrying a small brown-paper bag, most likely filled with a gift bottle of ouzo from my father, caught sight of Chance standing by the counter. And Chance returned the gaze, unblinkingly. From the look on both of their faces, neither had forgotten their tense introduction at the Thai place last Friday night.

I certainly hadn't.

Grant, not surprisingly, spoke first. "Personal trainer

guy, right?" he said, pointing at Chance.

Chance opened his mouth, closed it again, and then smiled tightly. "Chicago business guy, right?" he replied, mimicking Grant's intonation and body language, right down to the finger pointing.

Holy moly. Men and their caveman games of alpha dogging.

Grant's laugh was pure fakery. He sounded like an asshat at a cocktail party when he said, "You really get around in this town. Visiting all the hotspots, huh?"

And Chance was no better when he widened his stance and shot back, "Yeah, we Michaelsens are known to be omnipresent here in Mirabelle Harbor."

Mama nudged me hard and said, "Well, kids! You should get going. You don't want to miss the concert, do you?"

"No, we don't, ma'am," Grant said, walking toward me and touching my arm with an unmistakable gesture of possessiveness.

Chance stared at me from a few yards away, taking in the situation, and silently willing me to say *anything* that would in some way justify why I was going out on a date with another man...after I'd spent all of last night in bed with *him*.

Explanations needed to be made, I knew. But here and now, in the middle of my parents' bakery, wasn't the time or the place.

"I—" I began. "I just need to gather my things, Grant. How about I meet you in the car in a few moments, okay?"

Grant Jordan was an extremely successful businessman. I knew he recognized this as a relationship chess match of some sort. I also knew he was the type who played everything to win. Since I was leaving the bakery with him, and with my parents' blessing at that, the logical conclusion was that he must be the victor. That was how most games were played.

So he nodded at me in a show of graciousness and confidence as he walked toward the door. He sent Chance another faux grin, then waved more genuinely to my family, thanking them for their hospitality. "My car is just a few spaces down, Nia. The silver Mercedes," he added unnecessarily and a bit too smugly, I thought.

"Okay," I said.

My father wandered in the backroom, now that Grant was gone. My mother busied herself with cutting a tray of *pastichio,* a Greek variant of lasagna, into one-serving squares. And my brother looked deeply preoccupied with stacking imported jars of Kalamata olives on one of the shelves.

Chance crossed his arms, unmoving, and just waited for me.

I wanted to speak, but I needed to get him alone. "You know, your sister had been asking about the *amygdalota,* the almond cookies, the last time she was in here. Could you please give a small sample to her from me?"

Chance narrowed his eyes.

"It's right here in the kitchen," I said, waving him over, so he'd follow me. Reluctantly, he did.

I firmly shut the door between the kitchen and the bakery and then closed the gap between Chance and me.

I wrapped my arms around him but, though I could hear his heart beating through his shirt, he stood as still and straight as a steel rod. So, I stepped back.

"Chance, I have to go in just a minute. I need to—"

"What the hell are you doing, Nia?"

"I have to talk with Grant, okay? I didn't expect him to show up here today. I didn't expect you either."

"You said he wasn't your boyfriend anymore. Last night. In the sauna. Remember?"

Oh, yeah. I remembered.

"Yes, Chance, and that's true...for *me*. But I didn't have time to tell him that myself. I just left his place last night.

You knew that. You helped me with my escape."

He nodded curtly. "And your family? It seems they're also unaware of your change of heart."

"My family is...well, it's complicated with them. They really like Grant. I don't know that they'll understand how I might suddenly be with you rather than with him."

"*Why* wouldn't they understand that?" he asked, his voice as stiff and unyielding as his posture.

"Because they don't know you yet. To them, it would seem very sudden and surprising. Even though they just met Grant for the first time last week, they've heard a lot about him over the past couple of months. And he's been really good with them. They've gotten kind of...attached."

"So, let me recap. You're saying Grant doesn't know that he's no longer your boyfriend. Your parents and your brother don't know that you've only *mentally* broken up with him. But they all like the guy and want the two of you to be together, so you've continued to let them think you're still a couple. And tonight you're going out with him...why was that?"

"Because I have to break up with him in person."

Chance pointed in the direction of the street. "He's parked just a few spaces away," he said with a clear mocking tone. "Can't you talk to him in person in the safety of downtown Mirabelle Harbor? Do you have to go somewhere else where if, let's say, he gets mad about this breakup, he could leave you stranded?"

"Grant wouldn't do that. He's a decent guy—"

He cut me off with a disbelieving shake of his head. "Tell me something, Nia. Truthfully. Is there an *us* in the real world, or are you having second thoughts?"

"Chance, you have to know—you must know, especially after last night—that I can't continue dating Grant, no matter how much my family wants me to. But I need to be fair to him—"

He laughed without a trace of humor. "You need to be

fair to *him?* See, that's one of the things that really confuses me. Where, exactly, are your loyalties? Because you talk about Grant. And you talk about your family. But you don't seem to be factoring me into that equation anywhere."

I sighed in frustration. "Of course you're in there. You're the *reason* for all of this change. Don't you get it? I'm trying to make things right, so we can be together, but your unfamiliarity with my family's heritage makes everything a lot harder. One thing my parents like about Grant is that he knows how to act around them. It's instinctive for him. But you're someone new to them. Someone very different. And it's going to be much more difficult to get them to accept you as a boyfriend for me."

He went motionless, expressionless as he processed what I'd just said. I was hoping he'd take a deep breath. That he'd understand the delicate balance I was trying to manage here. But he came to a completely different conclusion.

"Well, damn," he said, his voice low. "I'm an idiot for not seeing this sooner."

"Seeing what? What are you talking about?"

"Your parents. You keep talking about your parents, how much they *really* like Grant. How you need to be so very careful about how you introduce me to them. How you'll have to control their impressions of me. What you're really saying is that your parents won't think I'm good enough for you. That I'm someone you're attracted to, someone you'll have sex with—late at night, in secret, when no one else will know about it. But I'm not someone you want to openly introduce to them as your boyfriend anytime soon."

"No, that's not true—"

"Not true at all? Or only *partially* not true?"

"Chance, all I've been saying is that it's going to take a little more time with them. To win them over. To get them to know you like I do."

He shook his head. "I don't think so. I think this is about a lot more than timing. It's not just about you breaking up with Grant in a 'fair' way, is it? Or easing me into your parents' circle of acquaintance. It has to do with your perception of us as a couple. How you don't see us as matching somehow. How you don't feel I'll ever fit in with your family. And, most of all, how you'd much rather not be honest with me about it. Or with your parents. Or especially with yourself."

I didn't know what to say to that. He *wouldn't* fit in with my family...not easily. It would take a lot of time to get them to accept him and, with certain relatives, it might not ever happen. Which didn't mean we shouldn't try. It was just confusing to me, and there was so much pressure put on choosing the *right* relationship.

Chance apparently took my silence as my response. For someone who didn't express a lot of emotion as a rule, he managed to look both very hurt and very mad at the same time.

Instinctively, I reached out to touch him. To try again to connect and explain.

He brushed me off, shuttered his emotions, and pointed to the array sharp utensils on the kitchen counter. "How about the next time you want to gut me, Nia, you just use a knife and be done with it, okay? It'd be less painful."

Then he yanked open the door to the bakery and stalked out.

Mama was in the backroom with my father, but my brother sent me a disapproving look as we watched Chance leave The Gala. "He looks really pissed."

"No kidding, Dimitri," I said, grabbing my purse and a light jacket, and then going outside to find Grant and his fancy car.

CHAPTER TEN

~*Chance*~

It took a helluva lot to make me angry.

Right now, leaving Nia at The Gala, I was angry. Really, *really* angry.

And so damn hurt that I wished I could let myself cry.

I tried walking down the street, but that didn't help. I wasn't moving fast enough, hard enough.

So I broke into a run, and I just kept going—through the downtown, past the schools, over to the lake, and along the shore. I ran until sweat dripped off me like I was under a water hose. Until I could stop wanting her for ten seconds. Stop wishing I could go back to last night and forget that today ever happened.

But today *did* happen.

And I was just going to have to live with that.

When I got home, I took a long shower and then called Blake.

"I'm a fool," I told my brother, and I relayed to him what went down at the bakery.

"Love makes fools of all of us," he said in his sage,

radio-station voice.

"Don't talk to me like that," I snapped. "Since when do you know anything about love anyway?"

"Song lyrics, Chance. I listen to lots and lots of romantic song lyrics. It's modern poetry."

"And besides, I don't *love* her. What I'm feeling is just an intense...infatuation."

Wasn't it?

"Really?" Blake said. "How many women have you ever been this 'infatuated' with in, say, the past decade?"

No one.

But I wasn't about to tell my brother that.

"You think she's really hot, right?" he continued. Then, without waiting for me to reply, he said, "Answer this question—to yourself, if not to me. Would you still be feeling hurt right now if she weren't so pretty?"

"What? Well, *yeah*. It's the principle of the thing! What do her looks have to do with it?"

"A lot, actually. If, as you said, this was just an infatuation. But you care about what she thinks of you. How her family sees you. You want to be involved in her life. You can imagine the two of you together for the longer term, right?"

"So? I've had crushes where I imagined marrying some other girl before," I said. I could hear the defensiveness in my own voice. Bet Blake could hear it, too.

"Did I say anything about marriage?" my brother asked. "Hmm, interesting. Listen, Chance, this is one of those 'do as I say and not as I do' situations, okay? I, personally, don't think relationships are worth the risk and the heartache. But it sounds like this chick might be worth it to *you*."

"She's not a *chick*. You know, don't call her—"

"Yeah," my brother said, cutting me off with a not-so-subtle snicker. "My point exactly. *Nia* means something to you. So, would you just stop pretending you don't care and, maybe, try to tell her that?"

I came to the conclusion that Blake wasn't being helpful, and I decided to call Derek.

"Relationships are about understanding and compromise," my married brother told me. "Were you really *listening* to what Nia was telling you?"

Jeez. "Yes, I was listening."

"Without judgment, Chance?"

That conversation was even shorter and less helpful than the one with Blake.

I figured only Chandler would know what I was talking about. He was my twin, dammit. He was supposed to understand me when no one else did. So, I called him. No answer, just his voicemail.

Usually, I let it ride when I got the automated recording. But I needed him. So, I left a message saying, "It's important, Chandler. Call me." Then I did a hundred crunches on the floor, about five hundred torso twists, and more pushups than I remembered to count.

Finally, my twin brother called me back. An hour later. And drunk.

"She's a woman and you're a man," Chandler slurred, after I attempted to explain the Nia Pappayiannis story to him.

"Yeah?"

"So, act like one!" my intoxicated twin instructed forcefully. "If she doesn't love you back, screw her. Or screw one of her friends. Or screw someone else you find at the bar...or the gym or wherever you like to go. Just don't let her screw with your head."

Unfortunately, this was the least helpful advice of all.

I hung up on my third brother of the night and thought, Oh, what the hell?

I'd tried every other sibling already. Might as well talk to Shar, too.

~*Nia*~

"Here's to you," Grant said, raising his wine glass. "And to a night of inspiring music."

"Thanks," I replied, clinking my glass with his and taking a sip.

Just as he'd promised, we were at an intimate Italian restaurant with good wine, great food, and an excellent atmosphere, just steps away from the concert hall on Chicago's north side. As always, he'd ordered more for us than we could eat—an antipasto platter, toasted ravioli, eggplant parmesan, chicken marsala with mushrooms—all of it delicious. I was having a hard time relaxing and enjoying it, though, after that confrontation with Chance back at The Gala.

He was *so* stubborn. And frustrating! And...and completely irrational about all of this. I'd been arguing with him in my head for the past hour and a half.

"Don't you like it?" Grant asked me, breaking into my thoughts.

I'd speared one of the toasted raviolis with my fork but hadn't bitten into it. From his viewpoint, it must have looked like I was studying it and finding it lacking in some way.

"Oh, no. It's wonderful." I forced myself to eat it immediately. "I was just wondering about the filling. A type of cheese, maybe?"

"We can ask our server," he said with a smile.

I smiled back and decided to make an effort to be more conversational. "So, do you often come to the Parkside Pavilion for concerts?"

"I've been to a fair number," he admitted. "Mostly with the corporation. We've held special functions onsite for our shareholders and their families."

"Mmm. Sounds nice," I said.

"It is. The musicians have played Beethoven, Vivaldi,

some Tchaikovsky."

I just nodded in response. As usual when I was with Grant, I found myself wishing I knew more about subjects that I didn't. Like shareholders. And classical music. As kind and gentlemanly as he'd always been, I could never shake the fact that I wasn't entirely at ease with him. Or with myself when I was with him.

"Have you attended any concerts recently?" he asked me.

"Not recently. And, um, not Tchaikovsky."

"Who then?"

"My friends and I went up to the Ravinia Festival to see the Goo Goo Dolls and Matchbox Twenty a couple of summer ago. We just had lawn seats, but we brought a picnic with us and blankets. And we sang along with the bands and danced with the thousands of other people there that night. It was packed."

"You enjoyed it?"

"Very much." Although I couldn't think of that music without also thinking of Chance. "Let Love In" was by the Goo Goo Dolls. And when that song was playing at the gym and Chance looked at me...

"Well," Grant said, considering, "maybe we can do something like that together this summer."

I wanted to just go along with it. Wanted to say to Grant, "Yeah, that'd be great."

But I couldn't.

Even though Chance had been absolutely ridiculous to expect me to suddenly tell everyone in the world that my relationship with Grant was over, Chance's words at The Gala about my not wanting to be honest with myself rang uncomfortably true. There was something I was beginning to realize I was feeling. It wasn't about Grant, though. Or about my family. Or even about Chance. It was about *me*, but I couldn't quite articulate it. I just knew that I needed to start by saying goodbye to Grant, and I needed to be courageous enough to do it now.

"Grant," I began. "I'm not sure how to explain this because I don't even understand how it happened myself, but I think it would be unfair to you if we kept dating." Oh, God, I couldn't believe I was really doing this. I hoped I could end things without hurting him.

He looked over at me in surprise. Then his expression hardened. "What's going on, Nia? Did I do something wrong?"

"No, you didn't," I said quickly, and I meant it. "This is truly about me, not you. You're a remarkable man, and you've been really amazing—both to me and to my family." I swallowed. He didn't need to know all the details, but he did deserve to know the truth. "I wasn't looking to meet anybody else once you and I started going out. I really wanted this relationship to be *it*. For you to be *the one*." I paused again. "But somebody else walked into my life, unexpectedly, and he just...he just changed everything."

"Personal trainer guy?" he guessed.

"Yes. I'm sorry, Grant."

He nodded. "Thought there was something weird in the air between you two."

I laughed a little to try to break the tension. "Yeah. 'Something weird' is probably a good descriptor."

Grant cracked a small smile, but he quickly turned serious again. I could see him thinking, remembering events that had happened, and reframing them in a new light. I watched him as the words I'd just said began to sink in. He might be wealthy, successful, and good looking, but he was also human. And competitive. I could tell that hearing there was another man in my life wasn't easy for him. He was angry, and he couldn't quite hide it.

"So, when exactly did you start seeing this guy?" he asked, his jaw tense.

"I haven't been 'seeing' him, Grant. Not outside of my

workout sessions." *Well, not until last night...*

"But he was hitting on you there? At the gym?"

"I wouldn't say he was hitting on me." *Although Grant would probably call it that.* "We would just talk—"

"About what?"

"Um..." What *did* we talk about? It wasn't the topic so much as the intensity of our eye contact. The unusual amount of attention Chance paid to everything I said or did. The way I'd been so attuned to his subtle mood changes. "Mostly good posture and abdominal exercises. A little bit about family. And music."

"Music, huh?" Grant scoffed. "Sorry, Nia, but he doesn't really strike me as an especially cultured guy. Music, art, literature—I don't know what insights he's got that would impress you, to be honest. But—" He shrugged. "Whatever. It's your life. Your choice."

"It is," I agreed. "Again, I'm really sorry things didn't work out better for us."

He just sighed and shook his head, as if he still couldn't believe I'd chosen Chance over him. It occurred to me that few women—if any—had ever broken up with Grant Jordan. I doubted he had much experience with being dumped, let alone coming in second for something. All things considered, he handled this disappointment fairly well. And after a long moment, he said, "I know. Me, too."

I let out the air I'd been holding in my lungs, relieved we'd gotten to this point without any real trauma. I knew that even if Grant's ego was a bit dented tonight, he'd get over it. Quickly. I could see him already pushing the incident aside, and moving on. Glancing at the waitress. At the other customers. At his phone. Perhaps he'd liked the idea or me or the thought of us as a couple, but he wasn't deeply attached to me any more than I was to him.

We sat in awkward silence for a few minutes longer, staring at our half-eaten Italian meal, before he pointed at the table. "We're not going to let all of this good food go to waste, are we?" He twisted his lips into a semblance of a smile. "Perhaps we should skip the concert but, unless you're desperate to leave right this second, I don't see why we can't finish our dinner together...just as friends."

I felt tears prick the corners of my eyes, due to both exhaustion and gratitude—probably in equal measure. I appreciated that Grant was trying so hard to be a good guy. He wasn't the *right* guy for me, but I did like him. Much more, in fact, as a friend than as a boyfriend.

This feeling made me reach across the table and squeeze his hand. "Thank you for being so gracious about this. Yes, I'd love to finish our dinner together."

Which we did. And when he drove me home, we hugged each other goodnight, and he said, "Good luck with it, Nia. And goodbye."

"Goodbye, Grant. Thank you, again."

And because it was far too early to go in the house and answer Mama's questions—and because I'd had enough emotional overload for one night and couldn't imagine facing Chance either—I just went for a long walk by myself. To think and clear my head, until I figured it would be safe to finally go home, slip inside undetected, and get some much-needed sleep.

Mama, however, had stayed awake, too.

Though she was someone who generally turned in to bed early, she was waiting for me—alone—in the living room when I walked in the door.

"Antonia," she said. "Why don't you come sit with me for a few minutes?"

Despite this being posed as a question, I knew it was a command, not a request.

It was after eleven p.m. and I was bone-tired but,

nevertheless, I walked in there and sat down on the chair across from her. I seriously needed to rethink this whole "living at home" thing. Maybe it was time to finally get my own apartment, eh?

"How are you?" I asked my mother.

"Me? I'm fine." She smiled carefully at me. "Although your boyfriend—the *first* one—seemed to think I'd been ill."

"Oh, about that—"

She waved off my explanation. "I don't need to know about that part. I've made up excuses to leave events before, too. But I want to know about the *other* part. What you've been doing with the second guy. That Michaelsen boy."

Chance Michaelsen was no *boy,* but I didn't think that would be the wisest thing I could say to start my defense. "Well, Chance is my personal trainer, so I see him three times a week at the gym. We've become, um, friends—"

My mother was shaking her head. "That look he gave you in the bakery? That was not the look of a friend, sweetheart. You know that."

I nodded. "You're right. We're more than friends...now. But that wasn't true until last night."

"Last night. After you left your date with Grant, yes?"

"Yes," I admitted.

"Does Grant know you have another boyfriend besides him?"

"He does now, Mama. I told him tonight. When I broke up with him."

My mother's eyebrows shot up in shock. "You're not dating Grant Jordan anymore?"

I shook my head. "I'm not."

"But your father actually liked *him,*" she said. "Dimitri, too. And your aunt and uncle. Even your cousin Nick. And me. He said my *triopitas* were 'delectable.'" She shrugged in confusion. "What's not to love about him?"

"I know. I'm sorry to disappoint you—and everyone. No doubt about it, Grant's a great guy. But Chance is, too."

"Then I'm not understanding something," Mama said. "Why leave a handsome man with a good business and a big future ahead of him for...for an exercise fanatic who won't eat my baklava? You think you'd really want to marry such a person?"

"Oh, Mama," I said, covering my eyes with my palms. My exhaustion and all of my pent-up frustrations with Chance were making me want to collapse into a puddle of tears in the middle of my parents' living room.

"Tell me what you like about this boy," my mother said gently. "It's okay, Antonia. I will listen."

So, I began to tell her about the Chance Michaelsen I'd been getting to know. The man who'd helped me ease my back pain. The man I'd often seen reaching out to others— like the elderly Mr. Alleghany, the young widow Julia Crane, the very enthusiastic but not very athletic Margot Dollinger, who sometimes had a session with Chance right before mine. How he was so kind to all of them. So patient and calm.

But I knew he was deeply passionate, too. And when I was with him, I not only felt as though I were more myself than I'd been with Grant or with previous boyfriends, but I also felt I was a stronger version of myself. A better, bolder, and braver one. Someone who needed to be more honest and open because he demanded that. Because he was paying such close attention to me.

"Even after just a couple of weeks of knowing him," I said, "he's changed my life. I don't pretend to understand how. I just know it's true."

My mother nodded. "Do you see yourself marrying him? This new person—Chance?"

I felt the strangest sense of panic when she asked that. It was a similar emotion to what I'd experienced back at the Italian restaurant with Grant, just before I ended our relationship. A realization that existed somewhere in my body, but I was having a hard time articulating it. I could *feel* it, though. Right there in the space between my mind and my soul.

And, suddenly, I knew what it was. My heart had stepped in and managed to translate the emotion into understanding.

"I don't want to get married," I blurted. "Not to Grant. Not to Chance. Not to anyone." Oh, God, the relief at finally saying it aloud! I hadn't realized how that fear was strangling me. Keeping me scared and silent.

"Ever?" Mama whispered, clutching her chest.

I thought about this for a long moment and consulted my deepest gut instinct before I spoke. Much as I liked Grant, I'd always sensed it would be wrong for us to get married, no matter how good the idea looked to everyone else. With Chance, all I knew for sure was that I was insanely attracted to him and curious to get to know him much more intimately (and not just in bed). But I'd need a crystal ball to be certain about actually marrying him and starting a family.

"I don't know," I answered honestly. "But I think there's been too much pressure on me about this. Too much worry about hurrying up to meet a man and get married, Mama. I'm only twenty-six. I'm not ready to be someone's wife, and I'm definitely not ready to be anybody's mother. I need...time. A lot more time."

There was something about the day of the bridal shower, getting that pink book at the bookstore, and all of the advice I'd read in it. Somewhere, in the middle of the "Fear" chapter, I'd realized I'd been looking for the wrong thing all the time. That, for me, it wasn't about finding the right man; it was about *being* the right woman at the right place in my life. And I wasn't at that place yet.

My mother seemed to be processing this new information about her daughter very, very quietly and seriously.

Finally, she stated, "I am too young to be a grandmother now anyway." She held her arms out to me, a nonverbal plea for me to go over and hug her. I did, and we held each other for a long moment. Then she whispered in my ear, "But maybe not forever. You'll think about marriage and children again in a couple of years, right?"

"Sure, Mama," I said. "Give me a year or two, and I'll reconsider the idea."

CHAPTER ELEVEN

~Chance~

"**I** think I want to marry her," I told my sister the next morning over coffee. "Seriously, Shar, I've never felt like this about anyone. I'm crazy about her."

"What? You've known her for, like, two weeks," she said, pouring more cream into her mug, in addition to the sugar she'd already put in there. We were at a corner table of Not the Same Old Grind, our town's best place for coffee. And chocolate-chip cookies, according to my sister, who liked cookies—a lot. Which was why she'd insisted we meet here instead of just taking a nice healthy walk on this Sunday morning. "It's too soon for you to be thinking like that," she concluded.

"No, it's not," I whispered. "Nia's the one." I was as sure of this as I was of my own name. I'd half fallen for her before we'd ever even met. I'd imprinted on her, like some species of bird or something, the first time I saw her walk by the gym. And Friday night in my apartment sealed the deal. She owned my heart.

How Nia felt, though, I could only guess. Especially

after yesterday and that whole fuckup at the bakery.

I was still mad about it. Far angrier at myself than at her because I'd been feeling so fiercely attached and protective of her. Because I'd wanted to challenge her and make her admit what I already knew to be true...that we belonged together. And because I was so easily hurt by the implication that her family wouldn't like me. I'd never been prone to insecurity. But then again, I'd never cared this much before. For once, the stakes were really high.

"Okay, Chance, let's say you're right. You two are perfect for each other. What's the issue that has you talking to *me* instead of to *her?* I mean, if you know everything already, why do you need my advice?"

"You don't need to be snotty about it."

My sister only rolled her eyes at me. "Just spill, will you?"

I took a few deep breaths, trying to think of how best to phrase it. I knew I had to tread carefully when it came to Sharlene. I intended to be honest, but she was sensitive to anything that smacked of infidelity in a relationship. Her ex-husband Stephen had made the mistake of cheating on her, and she'd kicked his ass to the curb the very day she found out. Blake, who'd stood up in their wedding, took it personally as well, and he gave the jerk a pair of black eyes for daring to mess with our sister. (But then, Blake kind of liked fighting.)

In any case, I didn't want Shar to know there was another guy involved. Grant Jordan—the dickhead—wasn't the real problem anyway, much as I wished I could blame him. I'd believed Nia when she said she was planning to break up with him. I guess I was just jealous that her family liked him so much and that they might be thinking I wasn't good enough for her.

"It's her parents," I told my sister. "Nia thinks it's going to take a really long time for them to like me. That it's 'complicated' and 'difficult' and shit like that. And I don't understand it."

Shar, to my annoyance, laughed. "Are you kidding? Mr. and Mrs. Pappayiannis are sweethearts. Have you ever talked with them?"

"Briefly."

"Were you on your best behavior, Chance? Or were you being your usual terse self?"

"Terse?" I repeated. "I was polite, of course. You know I'm not someone who...jabbers at people."

"Yeah, I know," she said. "But were you making an effort to be a bit more, um, effusive in your praise of things? You know, the fine food they serve at The Gala, the lovely atmosphere of their establishment, the wonderful qualities of their daughter?"

I stared at her. "What?"

She shook her head. "I didn't think so..."

"Look, I want to be real with Nia and with her family. I'm not going to act all superficial and pretend I'm someone I'm not. That would backfire in the long run anyway. I mean, I'm not a billionaire, but I have a decent income. I live simply by choice. Maybe that doesn't come across as successful enough to them, but would they rather I tried to buy their daughter's affection? That would be ridiculous. And I don't dress in designer suits because I prefer to wear sweats and sneakers, and that's what's required for my job. But maybe that's not flashy enough. It's not like I refuse to dress appropriately for formal situations, but when I'm just walking around through the middle of town, I'm not going to—"

"Whoa, Chance, slow down and take your pulse or something. I don't think I've ever heard you rant for this long about anything."

I started to stand up. "Sharlene—"

"Just listen to me for five seconds, okay?" She paused and waited for me to sit back down.

"Your brothers and I—*we* all know your emotions run

deep. But someone who's a new acquaintance, like Nia's mom or dad, or someone in town who hasn't known you for half their lives, they might mistake your desire to be *genuine* for standoffishness or extreme reserve."

"Because I'm not always hugging people or getting in their face by kissing their cheeks or slapping their backs or acting all excited about some kind of pastry or something?" The direction of this conversation was starting to really tick me off.

My sister nodded slowly. "Yes. And keep in mind, Nia's family is Greek and quite traditional. She and her brother are first-generation Americans. You need to take her upbringing into consideration. Learn to understand and respect the culture. The cheek kissing and the back slapping and the food excitement, those are all signs of welcoming and openness. If you ever want to have a hope of being included in her family, you can't dismiss her heritage and customs. It's a big part of who she is."

I thought back to that day at the gym when Nia brought in that spinach pie—the *spanakopita*—for me to taste. It had meant a lot to her that I was willing to try it, and it seemed to make her happy that I'd liked it. A kind of acceptance, I guess. "Okay, that makes some sense," I admitted.

Shar smiled. "Glad to hear it. You know, you're not that far off track. You can still be real with Nia and her family. It sounds like what you feel for her is completely sincere, right? So, you just need to show your emotions in a way that she and her parents will be able to recognize and read clearly. Maybe consider *amplifying* your emotions a little, so that they'll be slightly more obvious. I know you prefer being the strong, silent, and extraordinarily subtle type, but..."

I actually laughed at this. Perhaps my sister had a small but valid point. Although I would have felt better if Nia had at least tried to call me or text me or something. Last night.

Or this morning. Anything to show me that she cared, too.

Shar's eyes were suddenly misty, though, and I didn't know why at first. Then she said, "I miss our parents a lot. With Mother's Day coming up so soon, I'm especially missing Mom right now. But I know how proud she'd be to see you finally opening yourself up to love, Chance. You and Chandler always had such different ways of dealing with everything—especially grief. Even as kids. Our brother would express every fleeting feeling, but you tended to keep so much to yourself."

I nodded. She was right about that as well.

"So I know your willingness to risk emotion now is a big step for you," she said. "Maybe take some time for yourself, if you need it, to figure out exactly what you feel for Nia and how to say it to her. Then meet up with her privately and lay it all out. You can't expect her to be able to just read your mind, like we do." She paused and added more sugar to her coffee, which totally didn't need any additional sweetening. But I knew better than to tell Shar something like that. She'd throw the sugar bowl at me.

This talk about the loss of our parents made me think of Shar's newly widowed friend, Julia Crane. So I asked, "How Julia been doing? What's it been, four months since Dr. Crane died?"

"Almost five," my sister said. "She's holding her own, but it's been really hard. I've got some plans for her for this summer, though, when her daughter's away at camp. Julia needs to get out soon. Meet some new people."

Shar's answer to almost everything was to 'get people together,' so I wasn't at all surprised when she told me she had a Michaelsen family gathering planned for the upcoming weekend.

"Friday night, my place," she said. "We're just going to talk and have pizza and beer. Be there."

"Fine," I said, though I couldn't guarantee how much I'd feel like talking.

Then she asked me about my twin...the one who was currently roaming around the East Coast, where, in Shar's opinion, he didn't belong. "Anything new from Chandler?" she said. "Has he called or texted?"

"Talked to him last night," I reluctantly admitted. I didn't lie to my siblings, even when it would be preferable.

Her brows rose. "And?"

"And he was drunk. Somewhere in the middle of Georgia."

"Damn," she muttered. "We need to get that guy to come home to us."

"I know, Sis. I know." And I was speaking the truth, but I had no freakin' idea how we'd get him back to Mirabelle Harbor anytime soon.

❀❀❀

After spending the morning with my sister, I went to the gym so I could think while working out. I did some lifting, some stair-stepping, some running, and a bunch of other exercises in an attempt to get a clear head.

It wasn't working. Not indoors. And especially not with so many things around that reminded me of Nia. The treadmills. The hand weights. The exercise balls. The sauna.

Much as I wanted to see her tomorrow afternoon for her session, the idea of trying to be a good fitness instructor for her while I was still so unsure of what to say left me with a sucky, uncomfortable feeling in the pit of my stomach. I needed to be prepared this time so I wouldn't screw up again.

Besides that, I always felt it was best to keep professional relationships and personal ones separate. In all good conscience—and because I wanted a *very* personal relationship with Nia—I didn't feel it was right to continue on as her trainer anyway. So, I asked a fellow trainer at the gym, who was currently free during that time, to take on the last few sessions with her. I also knew I needed to do something else.

"Three days off?" Gillian said at the front desk when I handed in my vacation request form. *"You?* I don't think you've taken even *one* vacation day since I started working here. Two-and-a-half *years* ago. What are you doing? Planning to run a marathon in Australia or something?"

I leveled my least friendly stare at her and shook my head.

She just laughed. "I'm serious, though! Where the hell are you going? Everyone will want to know."

"Just taking time to commune with nature," I said sarcastically.

"Hiking? Biking?" she guessed.

"A little of both." *And a lot of thinking.*

"All right. Well, we've got a few trainers open to subbing, so it shouldn't be a problem getting some people lined up for you. Have fun, Chance."

"Thanks."

~*Nia*~

I arrived at the gym five minutes before my usual two o'clock workout time on Monday afternoon. I'd been looking forward to seeing Chance again in person. There was a lot we needed to discuss, not the least of which was the tension between us during our conversation at The Gala on Saturday.

Yesterday, I'd almost called him. To tell him about my official breakup with Grant. And that I'd talked to my mother about how much I liked him. And that the marriage pressure thing was a big part of what had me so on edge.

But I chickened out.

Chance seemed like the type of guy who needed to cool

down in his own time before he could talk to anyone. And I figured I would just play things by ear based on how he handled our session today. Would he be all business? Or would there be a glimmer of that quiet passion I'd come to recognize in those golden eyes of his?

Turned out, it was neither. He wasn't there.

"But *where* is he?" I asked the lady at the desk. Gillian.

"In the wilderness," she said with an eye roll. "He's 'communing with nature,' or so he said."

Since when? He hadn't told me he was going anywhere.

"When will he be back? Tomorrow? Wednesday?" He wasn't going to miss *two* of our sessions, was he?

She shook her head. "Not 'til Thursday, but Chance already set you up with a new personal trainer." She shot me a friendly grin, as if I should consider this news a good thing, rather than a grave disappointment. "Here, I'll introduce you to him. Smike!" she called.

And a bald and burly 350-pound man emerged from the employees' lounge. He was built like a locomotive, and he didn't even crack a smile when he saw me. "Hello, Nia," he said, reaching out to shake my hand. "I'm Smike. That's short for 'Small Mike.' I'm the little guy in my family." Then he sort of smiled—finally.

I nodded. Okay, he wasn't Chance Michaelsen, but he seemed nice enough. I could handle this. "Hi, Smike," I said. "It's great to meet you. So, we'll be working together today and Wednesday, right? Until Chance returns?"

"Nope. I'll be finishing out the rest of your sessions. Chance made an alternate arrangement for you."

"W-What? But why?" I squeaked out.

Smike tilted his shaved head. "Don't know. He just told me he felt I'd be a better fit for you as a trainer. That you should have consistency for the second half of your program. But don't worry. I've got his notes." He patted the clipboard in his hand. "Says here you need to do some work with the five-pound free weights first. And that you're not a fan of the reverse fly, so we should minimize that one."

It made my heart ache that Chance remembered personal things about me. That he'd taken the time to write them down so his colleague would know that, too. But, most of all, I wanted to cry because he wasn't here with me. Because our last conversation had been one where he'd been so mad and so hurt that he'd stormed out. Uncharacteristic of him, I knew. And because I'd been too cowardly to call him yesterday when I'd had the opportunity. It hadn't occurred to me that he might just...leave.

Somehow, I muddled through the workout session, but I spent all of it on the verge of tears. And when the DJ on the radio—Chance's brother—played an Andrew Lloyd Webber love duet, "Only You," I almost broke down in the middle of the Nautilus section.

When I got home, I barricaded myself in my bedroom and, like a high-school girl who had a crush on a boy who was playing hard to get, I tried calling his apartment. (No answer, of course.) Then his cell phone. (It went straight to voicemail.) And then texting him. (Which got no reply, even several hours later.)

And I had to face the horrible truth that I'd foolishly taken Chance for granted. I'd just expected him to be there whenever *I* was ready. Thought he'd be willing to wait for me until I said, "Hey, let's talk."

But he had every right to step away from me first— whether it was temporarily or permanently. And letting him do so was a stupid risk I hadn't known I'd been talking.

Finally, Tuesday night I got a reply text from him.

I've been thinking about you a lot, Nia. And you're right. We have some things we need to talk about. I don't know when I'll get home tomorrow, but it'll probably be late, and I have to work early on Thursday. Are you free Thursday night?

I was so glad to hear from him, I would have made myself free ANY night...or morning...or afternoon...

I wrote, *Yes! Where? And what time?*

Had to admit, I was hoping he'd say his apartment. Or the sauna at the gym. Some sign that he wanted our reunion to be romantic in nature. But he went for a more neutral location than either of those.

How about the lake? Barrett's Pier. Six o'clock.

Barrett's Pier was a popular teen make-out spot after dark. Not at six p.m., though.

Nevertheless, I agreed, and then had to spend the next forty-eight hours waiting to find out what the hell was going on inside Chance Michaelsen's mind.

CHAPTER TWELVE

~Chance~

Nia was waiting for me at the pier when I got there.

For a moment, before she saw me, I just watched her as she strolled along those wooden slats with the lake as a backdrop behind her. So beautiful. I took a mental photograph, hoped for the best, and walked toward her.

She turned and saw me. "Chance. You're here." Her voice was soft and almost surprised, like she'd been holding her breath.

"Of course." I swallowed. For all the time I'd spent thinking about the exact words I'd say and their exact order, my throat closed up and my mind blanked out. I couldn't remember my opening line, and I didn't have a clue how to interpret the look she was giving me. It seemed wary and worried. But why? I was the one who should be nervous.

Then she said, "I've missed you."

That I could answer. "I've missed you, too, Nia. A lot." I paused and some of the phrases I'd planned to say started to come back to me. "I'm sorry about Saturday. I didn't

129

want to talk to you again too soon and make another mistake. So, I went up to Wisconsin to bike some trails and to think about us."

"And, um, what sort of thoughts about us were you having?" she asked.

I noticed her hands were white and sort of shaky, so I reached for them. They were not only trembling, they were cold. "Are you okay?"

She shook her head. "Not really." She paused but she didn't step away from me. She still let me hold her hands in mine. "I'm very sorry about Saturday, too, Chance. But please just tell me what you've been thinking—so I know."

"All right. Well, it's simple, really," I said, which was the honest-to-God truth. I'd known this part even before I'd left on my trip. "I'm falling in love with you."

Her dark eyes grew wide, as if she totally hadn't expected me to say that. But the hell with expectations. I wasn't going to pretend this wasn't true. I needed to tell her the rest of it, though, too.

"I'm not a person who talks just to hear the sound of my own voice, Nia, so I probably haven't answered every question you've ever had about me. But I'll tell you anything you want to know, and I won't lie to you. Ever. The thing is, in my whole life I've never felt such a strong connection with anyone. And it scares me to feel so much for you, so suddenly. I'm terrified that you might not feel the same way or that I might do something stupid and lose you. So—" I paused to gulp some air and prepare myself for whatever her reaction would be. "So, if you want to back away from me...if you think I'm not the right man for you and that your family will never approve of me...if you're looking for a completely different type of guy, then you should break this off now. Because my heart's involved, and it's only becoming more so."

She abruptly let go of my hands and then wrapped them around my body, her head against my chest. She was crying. No, more like *sobbing*. Oh, God. Did that mean it was over?

"Nia, it's all right. Everything will be okay." I didn't know how it would be okay for *me,* but she was so upset, and I was worried about her. I stroked her hair. "Please don't be sad."

She shook her head and finally spoke. "I'm *crazy* about you, Chance Michaelsen. Don't you dare tell me that it's all right if I just walk away from you. I don't want to walk away, do you understand?"

Truthfully, I didn't quite understand at first. All of those tears. All of that trembling. If I'd been forced to place a bet, I'd have guessed she wanted to sprint as fast and as far away from me as possible. Sometimes really emotional people just confused me. But she held onto me even tighter. And sort of pounded her small fists against my back in emphasis until her words finally sank in.

"You're crazy about me?" I repeated.

"Yes," she said to my chest. I was sure she could hear my heart pounding. It was so loud and insistent, even I could hear it.

This was a *good* thing. My heart pounded even harder. "When did you come to that conclusion?"

She dried her eyes on my shirt and looked up at me. "You remember the Easter Egg Hunt?"

I nodded. How could I forget?

"It started then," she said. "It never stopped, even when I wanted it to. And every day that I got to know you better, any stupid arguments I had for why we shouldn't be together began to crumble."

"Which arguments?"

"Like that you'd dated Donna. I was kind of jealous of that. That you'd been with her before me. That you two were, maybe, intimate," she admitted.

"I never slept with Donna," I told her. *Why would I sleep with Donna?* "And I had more reason to be jealous of that A-hole Grant Jordan than you did to be jealous of your old high-school friend."

"I never slept with Grant," she murmured. "I never even wanted to. You told me I needed to be honest with myself, so here's the truth, Chance. There was never any competition between you and Grant. The second I started listening to what my heart was saying, I ended up texting you...in the sauna with you...and then in your apartment...and then here by the lake. This is where I want to be. You're who I want to be with."

"What about your family, Nia? If you stay with me, you need to know that I want it to be forever."

"Forever is a long time."

I shrugged. "Not as long as this week was without you."

She laughed a little. "I'm a bit less worried about my parents' opinion on this now. I just got done convincing my mother that I didn't even want to think about getting married for a couple of years. And it's true...I don't. I'm not ready for marriage. With anyone."

I'd already thought about this, too, so I told her the truth as I saw it. "Well, I am. With you. Someone else might think it's too soon but, as my twin brother would say, 'Screw them.' When you're ready to get married, Nia, you let me know. I'm not going anywhere."

"You'll just wait?"

This seemed like stating the obvious to me, but I guess I had to practice saying some things aloud. "Yes. *For you,* I'll just wait."

Then she stood on her toes and brought her lips up to mine, and we made out on the pier like a pair of teenagers. And when the sunset came, we stood side by side, holding hands and watching the golden rays kiss the lake.

"Tomorrow night is a Michaelsen family get-together at my sister's place," I told Nia. "Just beer and pizza. And, uh, maybe some baklava or something."

"What?" She looked confused.

"I'd like you to come with me tomorrow," I said. "If you're free. And I'd like your help in picking out a few desserts at The Gala to bring along. Maybe a little basket with Greek pastries? I could use your advice. I know Shar would love it and...well, I'd like to try some of your family's specialties, too."

"You're kidding me, Chance."

"I'm not."

And I proved it to her when, later that night, she led me into the bakery and—right in front of her parents and her brother and a room full of customers—Nia set out a platter of pastries for us to taste test.

"You don't have to eat anything you don't want to," she whispered. But I did want to. I tried a forkful of every single one, selecting several types for the basket I was building.

I caught her parents exchanging a few cautious glances and her brother sizing me up. But then her mother smiled at me. I smiled back. Hey, it was a start. That was enough for now.

A few minutes later, her father offered me a complementary shot of this licorice-flavored booze, which was good but, man, it was strong.

"Ouzo," he told me.

I nodded. "I'd like to buy a bottle of that for the gathering, too," I said. I'd definitely have to keep a close eye on Blake while he was drinking it, but I knew my brother would be an instant fan of the stuff.

Mr. Pappyiannis grinned. He toasted me with the shot glass he was holding, said some other words in Greek that apparently meant "to your health," and then added, "Opa!"

And much, much later, at my apartment with Nia, she brought one small piece of her family's signature dessert into my bedroom. *Galaktoboureko.* I'd probably never learn to spell it, but I knew it was part custard, part phyllo dough, and coated in a light syrup.

She made me lie down.

Then she dipped her finger in the custard, ran it over my bottom lip, and kissed me. It was *all* sweetness.

Mmm. "This one's my favorite," I murmured.

"Mine, too," she said. And she did it again.

~*End*~

Up Next: *Look for Julia Crane's love story in the next Mirabelle Harbor book—**The One That I Want**—available July 26, 2015! Who will she end up with?*

EXCERPT: THE ONE THAT I WANT (MIRABELLE HARBOR, BOOK 2) – OUT NOW!

The summer after her beloved husband died in a car accident, Julia Meriwether Crane is still picking up the pieces of her life in Mirabelle Harbor and trying to help her ten-year-old daughter adjust to this difficult new reality.

After her best friend Sharlene—one of the well-connected Michaelsen siblings—talks her into finally going out on the town again, Julia finds herself stunned to be the object of interest of several different men: The boy who'd broken her heart back in high school. The college ex she'd left behind. And most surprising of all, the movie actor she'd always fantasized about but had never met in person...until now. Can one woman have more than one "great love" in the same lifetime? And, if so, how can she be sure which man that'll be?

Sometimes the person you think will be best for you isn't the one you really want. THE ONE THAT I WANT, a Mirabelle Harbor story.

From the Novel:

With the exception of my best friend Sharlene, the others in the wine bar had gone back to their conversations so, thankfully, I didn't have too many people witnessing my fumbles with setting up a (sort-of) date for the first time in twelve years. It was awkward, but I agreed to coffee with my old high-school boyfriend and gave Kristopher my phone number, which he dutifully punched into his cell so we could arrange a time and day to meet later.

Shar nudged me when he wasn't looking and whispered, "See? Not so hard, is it?"

I made a face at her and shrugged.

Finally, the party at The Lounge was beginning to break up. I was mentally congratulating myself on making it through the evening when the very sweet, well-dressed woman—Elsie was her name—wolf whistled. "Wait, people!"

Everyone halted.

"I've been wanting to tell you this good news all night." She paused for effect. "You know my friend Rosemary, the one who works at the Knightsbridge Theater in the city, right?"

Most of the group nodded, seeming to have met Elsie's friend or, at least, heard about her.

"There's a dress rehearsal for their upcoming summer production, 'The Bachelor Pad,' this Thursday at six-thirty in the evening, in advance of next Friday's Opening Night," Elsie said. "And Rosemary reserved a block of seats for us."

Despite the noise in the wine bar, an audible spike in sound came on the heels of those words, and a couple of the women actually squealed.

I squinted at them. I mean, tickets to a play were always nice, but wasn't this taking theatrical enthusiasm a bit far?

"But that's not all," Elsie continued enthusiastically. "Rosemary also got us passes to meet the cast, just as she did for that steampunk musical last year—"

"Steampunk musical?" I hissed in Shar's ear.

She nodded. "It was bizarre. Tell you more about it later."

I grinned and brought my glass of wine to my lips, draining it of its final swallow.

"—including a special Q&A session with the director, Zachary Leeward," Elsie added, "and with the star of the show, Dane Tyler."

I choked on the last drops of merlot, coughing so hard that Bill reached across the table to hand me a fresh glass of ice water, Shar patted me on the back, and everyone else stared at me worriedly. Except for Kristopher. He shot me a knowing look.

Yeah, of course he'd remember *that*.

"Are you okay?" Elsie asked me.

I gulped down half the water. *Oh, God. Of all the actors on the planet—Dane Tyler. Here? REALLY?*

My teen world had just materialized out of thin air, like that freaky phantom ship that came from absolutely nowhere in *Pirates of the Caribbean*. My gut twisted weirdly, and I could barely breathe. "P-Please go on," I managed to whisper.

She smiled. "So, if any of you want to go to the performance, and I know you do, let me know now, and I'll email the list of names to Rosemary in the morning."

Elsie was right. With the exception of one accountant guy, who had an out-of-town business trip next week, and a very disappointed single mom, whose kid was playing in a baseball tournament Thursday night, everyone else signed up to go.

Including *me,* at Shar's insistence. And including Kristopher.

My old high-school boyfriend leaned over the table and said with a laugh, "Well, isn't that something? Maybe, if you ask him real nice, he'll recite your favorite lines from your favorite movie to you."

"Ha," I said weakly.

"Which lines? Which movie?" Shar asked.

Before I could reply, Elise jumped in and pointed to Shar and then me. "You two want to ride down with me?"

Shar answered for both of us. "Oh, yeah!"

Although I managed to stop tripping over my own tongue and was able to thank the kind woman, I didn't succeed in making more than a few last bits of small talk. All I could do was blush furiously and think to myself, in the fevered squeaking of an adolescent schoolgirl, *OMG, I'm finally going to see Dane Tyler in person! Maybe even talk to him!*

In just one evening, three distinct memories of men from my past played out like a warped summertime version of *A Christmas Carol* in my mind. Haunting memories of relationships that I'd had or had lost or had wanted— sometimes simultaneously and always more powerfully than I'd expected—were reeling through my brain on a continuous loop, braiding my emotions with the mental film footage.

Before my best friend could ask me any more questions I didn't want to answer, I hugged her goodnight and raced into the evening, forgetting until my feet hit the pavement and I collapsed into the driver's seat of my car that I wasn't, in fact, lost in time.

That I wasn't living out some high-school fantasy.

That I wasn't a vulnerable young woman, helpless in the face of fate.

I started the engine, replayed those last three thoughts again, and shook my head.

Like hell I wasn't.

Learn more about the Mirabelle Harbor books on Marilyn's website page for the series:
www.marilynbrant.com/books/the-mirabelle-harbor-series

COMING SOON: YOU GIVE LOVE A BAD NAME (MIRABELLE HARBOR – BOOK 3)

About the Book:

"Nothing but love, 24/7" is the slogan of Mirabelle Harbor's only radio station, 102.5 "LOVE" FM. At age thirty-four, local DJ Blake Michaelsen is well-known for several reasons: his very sexy on-air voice, his omnipresent family, his eligible bachelor status, and his reputation as one of the most impulsive men in Chicago's northern suburbs.

High-school French teacher and lifelong romantic Vicky Bernier is not at all wild about people who exhibit reckless conduct. (Blake.) Or men who have gigantic egos. (Blake.) Or grownups who still act like teenagers. (Blake, again.) She deals with enough adolescent behavior during the school day. Unfortunately, she's the staff advisor to the Homecoming Committee, and they've chosen him as their DJ for the big fall dance.

What happens when a man whose job it is to play love songs for a living is forced to admit his deepest secret—that he doesn't believe in true love—only to discover that the one woman who might capture his heart is the same woman who distrusts him the most?

No matter what you call it, with love there's an exception to every rule. YOU GIVE LOVE A BAD NAME, a Mirabelle Harbor story.

SERIES CONNECTION: ON ANY GIVEN SUNDAE (SWEET TEMPTATIONS, BOOK 1)

Readers who are familiar with the stories in THE SWEET TEMPTATIONS COLLECTION (a trio of light romantic comedies set in the Midwest) might recognize references to the fictional Chicago restaurant "The Playbook," which is owned by Roberto Gabinarri, the hero of Marilyn's *New York Times* & *USA Today* bestselling novel ON ANY GIVEN SUNDAE. Also featured in the story is Nia's cousin Nick... Here's a brief description and a short excerpt from the book:

When Elizabeth's uncle Siegfried and Rob's uncle Pauly rush off to Europe for a month in summer, they temporarily relinquish the reins of their ice cream shop to their respective niece and nephew—two people who may have grown up practically next door to each other but who have next to nothing in common...

Rob Gabinarri was enjoying the sound of his own voice in his latest battle of wits with Miguel, the style consultant for his Chicago restaurant, when the phone rang.

"Rob Gabinarri, proprietor. The Playbook," he said into the receiver, feeling the usual pride at the words. He never got tired of announcing his ownership of this place.

"Roberto!" his uncle Pauly said.

Rob checked the date. It wasn't his birthday. It wasn't Christmas. It wasn't the NFL Playoffs or anytime close to the Super Bowl. Something must be wrong with somebody.

"Uncle Pauly, how are you? Is everything all right in Wilmington Bay?"

"Great, great."

"Everyone in the family? Mama and Tony and Maria-Louisa and the kids and—"

"Oh, they're all fine. Just fine. But I need your help."

This stopped Rob cold. The last time his independent uncle had asked for anybody's help, big hair and legwarmers had still been in fashion. No matter what, there was no way Rob could decline. Family always came first.

"Of course. What do you need?"

"You're the boss of that hotshot restaurant, right?"

"Right," Rob said, his pride wavering a bit as apprehension seeped in.

"You make the rules and set the schedules, right?"

"Right."

"So, what you say is what goes, right?"

The last of his pride was now replaced by full-fledged anxiety. "Uh, right."

"So, you could take some time off now, couldn't you, Roberto?"

"I, well…sure. I guess so, but…" *Please, please don't tell me I need to leave the safety of downtown Chicago and return to suffocating small-town Wilmington Bay. Please, no.*

"I need you to come back to Wilmington Bay for a coupla weeks. Help us out here in the shop."

Damn! "I—well, I'm not so good with sweets, Uncle Pauly. Is there anything I can do for you from here? Anything I could send up? Supplies, maybe? I could hire a person who could step in for a while and—"

"*Dire sciocchezze.* You're talking nonsense, boy. You're great with sweets, and we need *you*."

Rob stifled a heavy sigh. "Okay. When do you need me?"

There was a pause on the line. "Is three hours too

soon?" his uncle asked, his brusque voice unusually cheerful. "How about four?"

Available in ebook, paperback, and audiobook!

"Marilyn Brant is a master at the fast paced modern romance. Very cute tale with lots of laughs. Great read."
~Reviewer Jen Red, *On Any Given Sundae*

ABOUT THE AUTHOR

Marilyn Brant has been told she writes with honesty, liveliness and wit (descriptors she's grown terribly fond of) about complex, intelligent women—like her friends—and their significant personal relationships. Although her favorite pursuits undoubtedly involve books, she proves she's not just a literary snob by confessing her lifelong fascination (read: obsession) with popular music, especially from the '70s and '80s, most flavors of ice cream, and a variety of sensuous body lotions/oils.

As a former teacher, library staff member, freelance magazine writer and national book reviewer, Marilyn has spent much of her life lost in literature. She is the *New York Times* and *USA Today* bestselling and award-winning author of nine novels to date, and a lifetime member of the Jane Austen Society of North America. The Illinois Association of Teachers of English (IATE) selected her as their 2013 Author of the Year.

Her debut coming-of-age novel, *ACCORDING TO JANE* (Kensington, 2009), featuring the ghost of Jane Austen giving a young woman dating advice, won the Romance Writers of America's prestigious Golden Heart® Award and the Booksellers' Best, and it was named one of the "Top 100 Romance Novels of All Time" by Buzzle.com. Her second novel, *FRIDAY MORNINGS AT NINE* (Kensington, 2010), was a Doubleday and Book-of-the-Month Club pick in women's fiction. *A SUMMER IN EUROPE* (Kensington, 2011) was featured in the Literary Guild and BOMC2, and it became a Top 20 Bestseller in Fiction and Literature for the Rhapsody Book Club. The Polish translation of the novel was released in June 2013.

She's also a #1 Kindle and #1 Nook bestseller, who writes fun and flirty romantic comedies, like her stories in *THE SWEET TEMPTATIONS COLLECTION*, that involve sweet treats, unexpected love and large doses of humor. *THE ROAD TO YOU*—a coming-of-age romantic mystery—was selected as one of the Top 20 Best Books of the Year (December 2013) by The Reading Frenzy. Several of her novels will soon be available in audio CD/download from Post Hypnotic Press. Look for them in 2015 and beyond, and be sure to keep an eye out for more romances in the "Mirabelle Harbor" series, coming soon!

Marilyn currently lives in the Chicago suburbs with her family. When she isn't reading her friends' books or watching old movies, she's working on her next novel, eating chocolate indiscriminately and hiding from the laundry. Please visit her website: www.MarilynBrant.com.

www.ingramcontent.com/pod-product-compliance
Lightning Source LLC
Chambersburg PA
CBHW021100130626
46552CB00005B/2188